"You're not going anywhere," Paige said to the Anubi demon, holding a ball of fire over his face menacingly. "Not until you tell us what you've done with all the witches you've taken."

The Anubi let out a low, menacing laugh and a chill ran down Piper's spine. "They're all dead," he told them. "But we still have their blood if you're interested."

Piper's breath caught in her throat as the Anubi turned its massive head toward a line of more than twenty canisters on the windowsill. If each one held the blood of a different witch, then there were even more victims than they had thought. Suddenly, Piper felt her whole body go numb. She turned and looked at Tessa and Taryn who were huddled together by the door.

"That means that Tina is . . . Tina is actually . . ." Taryn took one step away from her sister and fainted, her body falling limp on the floor. Tessa crumbled next to her and started to sob.

Her heart twisting painfully, Piper turned slowly back to the Anubi, lifted her hands, and just as Phoebe, Cole, and Leo flung themselves out of harm's way, blew him to pieces.

More titles in the

Pocket Books series

All Pocket Books are available by post from:
Simon & Schuster Cash Sales. PO Box 29
Douglas, Isle of Man IM99 1BQ
Credit cards accepted.
Please telephone 01624 836000
fax 01624 670923
Internet http://www.bookpost.co.uk
or email: bookshop@enterprise.net for details

SOMETHING WICCAN THIS WAY COMES

An original novel by Emma Harrison

Based on the hit TV series created by

Constance M. Burge

POCKET
BOOKS

LONDON • SYDNEY • NEW YORK • TOKYO • TORONTO

For Liesa.
Happy birthday to my charmed friend.

First published in Great Britain in 2003 by Pocket Books.
An imprint of Simon & Schuster UK Ltd.
Africa House, 64–78 Kingsway, London WC2B 6AH

Originally published in 2003 by Simon Pulse,
an imprint of Simon & Schuster Children's Division, New York

ISBN 07434 62483

5 7 9 10 8 6

Printed by Cox & Wyman Ltd, Reading, Berkshire

SOMETHING WICCAN THIS WAY COMES

Chapter
1

"Viva Las Vegas! Viva . . . viva . . . Las Vegas!"
Paige Matthews sang to herself as she pulled her little green VW Bug up in front of Halliwell Manor on a beautiful Thursday evening.

The sun was just starting to set, painting the sky over San Francisco with streaks of bright pinks, purples, and yellows. It was Paige's favorite time of the day, when work was over and the whole world seemed to sigh with relief. But on this particular Thursday she'd been alternately singing and humming ever since the early afternoon. Unfortunately, she'd been singing the same three words over and over and over again because they were the only words she knew of the classic song. But Paige didn't care. She couldn't have stopped singing if she'd magically clamped her own mouth shut. She was just too excited.

1

Paige grabbed her crocheted bag and climbed out of the car, then took the steps up to the front door of Halliwell Manor two at a time. She had always wanted to go to Las Vegas—to see the Strip and all its lights and sights and sounds for herself. Maybe even score a huge jackpot. And now she was actually going! This time next week she would be there—playing the slots, cruising the casinos, winning some cash. . . .

If she could convince her sisters to come with her.

Paige's two older sisters, Piper and Phoebe Halliwell, had been a little less than sociable lately, what with all the demon fighting they'd been doing in the past few weeks. But that was part of the package when you were the Charmed Ones—the three good witches destined to protect the innocent from the forces of evil. Maybe things had been a little more demonic of late, but that could actually work in Paige's favor. She was going to stay positive and hope that her excitement would prove to be contagious. Her sisters wanted a vacation. They *needed* a vacation. They just didn't know it yet.

"Piper?! Phoebe?! Are you guys home?" Paige called out as she burst through the front door. She pulled a computer printout from her bag as she paused for an answer. The sound of hurried footsteps greeted her, and moments later Phoebe came barreling down the stairs, while

Piper rushed in from the kitchen. Both of them looked stressed and concerned.

"What is it?" Piper asked, pushing up the sleeves on her white peasant top. "What happened?"

"Nothing!" Paige said with a grin. "Everyone chill. I am not here to announce a brush with death, demon related or otherwise. Although this guy did cut me off on the freeway, and it was all I could do to keep from orbing him out to Alcatraz."

Piper and Phoebe exchanged a disturbed look, and Paige rolled her eyes.

"I would never actually *do* it, you guys," she said with a scoff.

And she wouldn't. Paige knew better than to use her powers as an outlet for road rage—or to vent any other emotion, for that matter. The Charmed Ones were not allowed to use their powers for personal gain. It had a way of back-firing when they tried. But there was nothing in the Book of Shadows that said they couldn't daydream.

"Okay, Paige, so what's up?" Phoebe asked, coming down the last few steps and sitting on the landing. She swung her dark brown ponytail over her shoulder and looked up at her younger sister. "What's with all the shouting?"

"It's good shouting," Paige said, putting her bag down on the floor near the stairs. "The best kind. See?" She held out the computer printout to Piper and smiled. "We're going on vacation!"

"We are?" Phoebe asked, her perfect eyebrows shooting up. She seemed psyched at the proposition, and Paige felt a little flicker of hope rise up in her chest. Maybe this would turn out to be an easy sell. Of course, she hadn't gotten to the part she was worried about yet. The part her sisters would probably have a hard time swallowing.

"No, we're not," Piper said flatly.

So much for the hope flicker.

Piper handed the page to Phoebe, who glanced over it quickly, then smirked.

"You're kidding me, right?" she said, holding the paper out in Paige's direction.

"Do I look like I'm kidding?" Paige asked. She gingerly took the printout back and looked down at it morosely. What was wrong with them? Didn't they see the potential for fun in the sun? For an enriching experience? For huge jackpots?

"You want us to go to a Gathering of the Covens?" Piper asked in a disdainful tone she usually reserved for talking about the troublemakers and drunks she sometimes had to have booted from her nightclub, P3.

When the sisters weren't fighting demons, they did have their day jobs. Piper ran the most popular nightclub in town, Phoebe wrote an advice column for one of the area's newspapers, and Paige was a social worker. Yet another reason why they needed a vacation. Technically they were each working two jobs!

"Yeah!" Paige said, her eyes wide. "What's so far-fetched about us going to a Gathering? We *are* witches, you know. We're, like, *the* witches."

"Exactly. And I'm guessing ninety percent of the people who show up at that thing don't know the first thing about the kind of evil we have to deal with on a daily basis," Phoebe said, standing up on the bottom stair. She pushed one hand into the pocket of her denim skirt and rested the other on the gleaming wooden banister.

"So? We don't know very much about the Wiccan religion or culture," Paige argued. "We spend most of our time vanquishing demons. Don't you want to know more about the craft behind what we do?"

"Paige, we know about the Craft," Piper said. "Or did you already forget the hours of potions studying we did when you first moved in here?"

Paige groaned. How could she forget the most torturous study sessions of her life? Piper had been like a drill sergeant when Paige first came to the manor, teaching her all about crystals and herbs and the various reptilian body parts that were used in spells and potions. Paige had found her sisters only recently, so she had a lot of Charmed learning to do to catch up. But there was so much more Paige wanted to know! Maybe she and her sisters were pros at throwing together vanquishing spells and conjuring protection crystals, but that didn't mean their knowledge of magic had to end there.

"How did you find out about this, anyway?" Piper asked, crossing her arms over her chest.

"It was slow at work this afternoon and I started surfing the Web," Paige said with a shrug. Her spirits were starting to deflate more with each passing moment. "You wouldn't believe how many covens have their own Web site."

Piper and Phoebe laughed, and Paige felt her face color. "I'm not saying we should go digital," she said, frustrated. "But it sounds so cool. The Gathering is going to be around the summer solstice, and there are all these rituals they perform to honor the Goddess. . . ."

Paige looked to Phoebe, hoping at least to find an ally in her middle sister. Phoebe had always been a little more into the spiritual, romantic, mystical side of things than Piper, who was all about practicality. But Phoebe was still looking at Paige with a skeptical expression in her big brown eyes.

"Besides, you guys, it's in *Las Vegas*!" Paige said, not willing to give up quite yet. "We could have so much fun!"

"That just makes it even more bizarre,"

Phoebe said. "If they're going out there to be all spiritual and commune with one another, why are they going to Sin City, of all places? I have this vision of chicks in black hats smoking cigars and playing craps."

Even Paige had to smirk at that mental image, but she quickly wiped it away.

"Piper—"

"I'm sorry, Paige, I just don't see the point," Piper said, running her hands through her light brown hair. "I mean, we're out there fighting evil every day. What do we have in common with a bunch of people whose idea of being a witch is casting magic circles and blessing their cats?"

"You're so judgmental," Paige grumbled, looking away.

She had no idea why she was letting herself grow so upset over getting shot down, when she'd suspected all along this was going to happen. She'd known Piper and Phoebe long enough to know that they were going to be skeptical about the Gathering. But she couldn't help it. She hated the fact that her sisters wouldn't even consider her plan. They had to be able to tell how excited she was. What was she supposed to do, go to this thing alone? *Not likely.* It was a Gathering of the Covens, not a Gathering of Lone Loser Witches.

"It's just not my idea of a vacation, sweetie," Piper added apologetically.

Paige wracked her brain for a good, convincing argument, but she couldn't find one. At least not one that would change the minds of the Stubborn Ones. That was what she was going to call her sisters from now on—the Stubborn Ones.

"Besides," Phoebe put in, "Cole and I just got engaged. I don't know if I want to leave him here while we go dancing around under a full moon with a bunch of phonies. Especially not with all the demons that have been popping up around the manor lately. Cole's human now, and there's no way he could defend himself."

"Well, Leo will be here," Paige argued. Piper's husband, Leo, was a Whitelighter, a kind of guardian angel who looked over the Charmed Ones and came whenever they needed help.

"But he can't be here all the time, and there's not much he can do to fight demons on his own," Piper pointed out.

"I can always orb us back here if I need to," Paige said.

"I don't know . . . ," Phoebe said, looking at the floor. "I just don't think it's a good idea."

Paige took a deep breath and pushed her dark hair behind her shoulders, trying not to look as disappointed as she felt. Usually when Paige got an idea like this in her head, she wouldn't give up until she got her way. But she could tell she wasn't going to get anywhere with this argument, and it was clear that Piper and Phoebe thought it was pretty much over anyway.

"Okay, fine," Paige said, crumpling the page up in one hand. "It was just an idea."

She picked up her bag and started up the stairs, brushing by Phoebe. She knew that Piper and Phoebe would probably start whispering about her in approximately five seconds—talking about whether she was really upset and if they'd handled the situation properly. It was what they did. And Paige didn't mind, really. She'd been on the other side of it many times. She just didn't want to catch one word of it.

As soon as she got to her bedroom, she closed the door behind her and cranked up her stereo. She kicked off her wedge sandals as she sat down on her bed, then tossed her crumpled-up vacation idea toward her garbage can. It missed by about three feet and hit the floor.

Frustrated, Paige thrust out her hand. "Paper," she said through her teeth. The ball of paper was engulfed in a swirl of blue white light, then appeared in Paige's hand again. She chucked it at the garbage can once more, this time executing a perfect basket. Then she flopped back on her bed and looked up at the ceiling.

"So much for viva-ing Las Vegas," Paige muttered.

"I feel kind of bad," Phoebe said quietly as she followed Piper across the living room and into the kitchen. "She was so excited."

She slid onto one of the stools at the center island and leaned her elbows against its cool surface. Part of her wanted to say yes to Paige's proposition simply because her little sister was clearly dying to go, but she just couldn't find it in her heart to share the excitement. There was a lot going on in Phoebe's life lately, and learning how to be a better Wiccan was not on the top of her priority list. Helping her soon-to-be husband find a job, writing her column at the paper, and staving off the demons had to come first.

"I know," Piper said with a sigh. "But Las Vegas with a bunch of wanna-be witches? I don't think so."

She poured out two cups of coffee and slid one across the tiled island to Phoebe.

"Mmmmm, but where would you go if you could go on vacation?" Phoebe asked, cradling her cup in both hands and drawing her arms in toward her chest as she took a sip of the hot coffee. "I mean, if you could go anywhere in the world?" she added, grinning as she started to daydream herself.

"Right now I'd definitely go for the islands,"

Piper said, tilting her head to one side and closing her eyes. "The warm sun, the gauzy clothes . . . the fruity drinks with umbrellas."

"And Leo, of course," Phoebe said with a knowing smile.

"Of course," Piper said, her eyes popping open. "Leo is a given." She took a sip of her coffee and looked at Phoebe. "Okay, now I'm salivating. Where's my husband when I need him to take me to the Bahamas?"

Suddenly a huge swirl of light appeared in the center of the kitchen, and when it disappeared, Leo stood there smiling and holding a tropical flower. "You called?" he said, sliding up to Piper's side.

"This whole Whitelighter thing can be so convenient sometimes," Piper said, standing on her tiptoes to kiss her husband. As a Whitelighter, Leo was able to orb from place to place and could always hear Piper and her sisters when they called for his help. Paige was half Whitelighter, half witch, so she could orb not only herself, but other objects as well.

Piper took the big pink flower from Leo's hand and twirled it between her fingers. "What would you say to a weekend on the beach?" she asked.

"I'd say it's long overdue," Leo replied, his blue eyes twinkling.

"Okay, you guys are making me miss my

man," Phoebe said, shifting in her seat.

"Where is Cole, anyway?" Leo asked.

"Job-hunting," Phoebe said with a grimace. "Let's just hope he has good news when he gets home."

As if on cue, Phoebe heard the front door open, and she put her coffee cup down and spun around in her seat, fully expecting to see Cole come striding through the door. But instead their friend Daryl Morris walked in, his forehead creased with worry and his necktie loosened uncharacteristically.

"Good, you're here," he said, rubbing his hands together as he looked from Phoebe to Piper and back again. Anxiety was coming off of him in waves. "Where's Paige?"

"She's upstairs," Phoebe answered as Daryl removed his jacket and took a deep breath. "Daryl, what's wrong?" she added. "You're freakin' me out a little here."

"I'll tell you once we get Paige down here," he said, going back out the way he came. As he called up the stairs for Paige, Phoebe shot Piper and Leo an alarmed look. Daryl was a detective with the San Francisco Police Department and the only civilian who knew about the sisters' powers. He didn't come to them in an agitated state unless he wanted to warn them about some major evil or to caution them because someone was becoming suspicious of them. Phoebe felt an unsettling churning in her stomach, and by the time Daryl returned with Paige, she'd managed to imagine about a hundred dreadful scenarios.

"What's going on, Daryl?" she asked, looking up at his dark, handsome features. "Spill, already."

"You're not gonna like this," he began, causing the little hairs on the back of Phoebe's neck to stand on end. "It looks like someone's been kidnapping practicing Wiccans."

"Here in San Francisco?" Paige asked.

"All over the country," Daryl replied, his tone serious.

"You're kidding," Piper said, shooting her sisters a disturbed glance.

"I wish I were," Daryl replied. He started to pace the room, as he often did when he had pent-up energy to expend. His well-shined shoes squeaked on the tile floor as he moved, and Phoebe almost got dizzy watching him.

"I was investigating a disappearance this morning and I was talking to one of the missing girl's friends," Daryl explained. "She tells me that the missing girl, Clarissa, was a member of a coven and that she and her sister witches were worried that something like this might happen. Turns out that this girl's cousin is in a coven back east, and there has been a rash of disappearances out there over the last couple of weeks."

"What defines a rash?" Piper asked.

"At least sixteen that I know if. Maybe more."
Daryl stopped pacing momentarily and pulled a
folded piece of paper from his breast pocket. He
flattened it out on the island, and Phoebe, Paige,
Leo, and Piper all leaned over it to read.

"'Attention Wiccans,'" Phoebe read aloud.
"'Please be on the alert! Wiccans are being kidnapped. We know of eight covens that have been
hit in the last few days from Boston to New York
to Virginia and as far south as Florida. The kidnappings often happen in the middle of the night
while the victim is sleeping. Please be aware of
your surroundings, lock up at night, invest in an
alarm system. *Do anything to protect yourself!* Let
us know if you hear of any more disturbing incidents. We have to protect one another. Your sisters and brothers need your help!'"

Phoebe felt a little chill run down her spine as
she looked at her sisters.

"Why haven't we heard about this?" Piper
demanded.

"Yeah. Where did you get this, Daryl?" Paige
asked, sliding the printout toward her.

"From this girl I was talking to this morning,"
Daryl replied. "Apparently it's been e-mailed
out to all the covens that are on the Web."

"And you don't want to go digital," Paige
said, shooting Piper a look.

"You said sixteen. This says eight," Piper

pointed out, ignoring Paige's comment.

"I did some digging and found some more," Daryl explained, running his hand over his short, dark hair. "A lot of these police departments didn't even make the Wicca connection, but this has happened in Texas, Chicago, Wisconsin. . . . It's almost like these sickos are working their way west."

"And now they're here," Phoebe said, her voice shaking slightly.

"There have already been three kidnappings in the Bay Area," Daryl said. He put his hands on his hips and blew out a sigh. "I just figured you guys should know. I mean, being who you are—"

"You could definitely be next," Leo put in, spelling out what every one of them was thinking.

"Do you know anything about the kidnapper?" Piper asked.

"Unfortunately, no," Daryl replied. "Each victim was taken in the middle of the night, like the e-mail says, but other than that and the Wicca thing, there's no evidence linking the crimes. Whoever's doing this is doing it clean."

"I'm gonna go check with the elders about this," Leo said, taking a step back from Piper. "They have to be concerned if this many Wiccans are missing."

"Let us know what you find out," Piper said.

"Of course," Leo replied, giving her a reassuring smile.

He orbed out, leaving the kitchen in an eerie state of silence. Phoebe looked at the e-mail warning, feeling another chill of foreboding. She couldn't imagine what it was like for these poor, innocent people, being snatched from their homes in the middle of the night. They must have been so scared.

"Daryl, is there anything we can do?" Phoebe asked, her adrenaline starting to kick in.

"Actually, I was hoping you'd offer," Daryl replied. "I don't want to put you guys in any danger, but if you could talk to a few of these covens in the area . . . I don't know, maybe they'll open up to you guys more easily. Maybe they know something and don't even realize it."

"Of course," Paige said, touching Daryl's arm. "We'd be happy to help."

"We'll do whatever we can," Piper added.

Phoebe took the e-mail page and stared down at it. A few of the words seemed to jump out at her: *kidnapped . . . protect . . . alert . . . help. . . .*

"We have to find out who's taking these people," Phoebe said grimly, leveling Paige, Piper, and Daryl with a determined glare. "And we have to do it before anyone else has to suffer."

Chapter

2

Piper sat down on the edge of an overstuffed couch in the middle of Missy Stark's living room, feeling completely conspicuous. She wasn't sure what bothered her about the place, but she felt as if she didn't belong. Missy had invited her in easily enough when Piper said the police had sent her, but she just couldn't get comfortable. The walls of the room were covered with dark blue wallpaper that had gold crescent moons printed all over it. Every window was hung with about ten thin, colorful drapes, and there were candles in different stages of meltdown on almost every surface.

Missy was in the kitchen making tea, and Piper could hear dishes rattling. She looked down at the table in front of her and noticed it was piled with books about witchcraft. *The*

Wiccan Year, Day by Day; A Guide to Crystals and the Power of Color; Your Coven and You. Piper smirked and it suddenly hit her. She was uncomfortable because Missy Stark was exactly the type of person she avoided—a touchy-feely Wiccan earth mother. Exactly the type of person that had kept Piper from taking Paige up on her Las Vegas trip.

Missy walked back into the room, her red ringlets catching the sunlight from the nearest window as she managed a wan smile. Piper's stomach turned dangerously as she realized there were dried tear streaks on Missy's face. Here she was making snap judgments about Missy, and she'd just lost one of her closest friends. It was time for Piper to focus on her purpose for being here.

"Thank you," Piper said as Missy placed a tray of teacups and butter cookies on top of her books on the table. She moved to the edge of her seat and crossed her legs at the knee. "So, you were going to tell me more about Clarissa."

"Oh! Let me find a picture!" Missy said, standing again before she even had time to hit the chair across the table. She seemed like a bundle of nerves as she flitted around the room, looking at framed photos on tables and on windowsills. "Here's one!" she said finally, picking up a silver frame that was decorated with pink and purple crystals.

Her flowy, flowered dress billowed behind her as she walked over to the couch and handed the frame to Piper. She took a few steps back, folding her hands and watching for Piper's reaction almost like a proud mother.

"Isn't she beautiful?" Missy asked. "Everyone she meets comments on that hair."

Piper held the frame gingerly between her fingertips. The first thought that popped into her mind when she looked at Clarissa's face was the word *angel*. Clarissa had pale, almost luminous skin. The lightest blond hair Piper had ever seen seemed to float around her face, and her bright blue eyes seemed happy and sorrowful at the same time.

"She's beautiful," Piper said, handing the picture back. Missy replaced the frame on the table where she'd found it and finally sat down across the coffee table from Piper. "You told the police that she disappeared in the middle of the night, is that right?" Piper asked.

"Yes," Missy said, leaning forward and pouring out two cups of tea from a flowered pot. "I talked to her right before bed around eleven o'clock. The next morning we were supposed to meet for an early breakfast, but she didn't answer the door when I got there. I know where she keeps her key, so I went to let myself in, but the lock was broken. I know I should have just called the police right then and there, but I had

to find out if she was okay, so I just went in. Her
bedroom was a mess, and there was a trail of
broken things down the steps and out of the
house . . . as if there had been a struggle."

Missy broke off and Piper held her breath,
hoping the woman wouldn't cry. Piper felt badly
for her and she wasn't sure what she'd say if
Missy lost control of her emotions. That everything was going to be okay? How could she say
that when they had no idea what had happened
to Clarissa? But Missy held it together. She
handed Piper a cup of tea and settled back into
her chair, balancing her own cup on its saucer.

A broken lock, Piper thought. *That sounds like a
human thing to do.* Demons could usually enter a
house without resorting to such rudimentary
tactics. Still, it could be that a demon was trying
to throw them off his trail. Some of them were
smart enough to mess with their own crime
scenes in order to do just that.

"I just don't understand it," Missy said. "She
didn't have any enemies, her family was very
supportive of her . . . everyone loved her."

"Maybe someone loved her too much," Piper
suggested before taking a sip of her tea. "Any
ex-boyfriends?"

Missy seemed startled by the question, as if it
was unthinkable. "No. Well . . . yes. She broke up
with Theo about a year ago, but it was totally

amicable. Besides, he's backpacking in Europe right now. She just got a postcard from him the other day."

So much for that, Piper thought. It had been a long shot anyway. It wasn't like Clarissa's ex was out there kidnapping Wiccans all over the place. "What about your coven?" she asked. "Any jealousy? A power struggle?"

"Well, Clarissa is our high priestess, so obviously she's in a position of power," Missy said with an easy smile. She took a long sip of her tea, then placed her cup and saucer down on the table. "But our coven is peaceful. We all get along, and Clarissa's ascension to the position was unanimously supported. The Goddess is strong in her."

Piper had to concentrate to keep from rolling her eyes. "What do you mean by that?" she asked, trying hard to keep all sarcasm out of her voice. It made her sound completely toneless.

"You're going to think I'm insane," Missy said, scoffing and looking away. She brought her thumb to her lips and chewed on the side, looking at Piper out of the corner of her eye.

"You can trust me," Piper said, leaning forward slightly. "I could tell you a lot of things that would probably make *you* think *I'm* insane."

Missy took a deep breath, her chest rising slowly as she considered Piper. "Okay, maybe it'll help, but I warned you," she said finally. Then she bit her lip and squeezed her eyes shut. "Clarissa can see things."

Piper saw a little red flag go up in her mind's eye. Maybe Clarissa and her friends weren't your run-of-the-mill Wiccans. Missy opened one eye as if she was afraid to see Piper's reaction.

"What kinds of things?" Piper asked point-blank.

"When she touches an object . . . any object . . . she can see the last person who touched it. Almost like a premonition or a vision," Missy explained, a hint of excitement in her voice. "She can even tell what they were feeling when they held that object, and can sometimes tell what they did next—after putting it down."

"Wow, that's some power," Piper said, clearing her throat as she put her cup down.

"Clarissa has always been able to sense emotions by touching objects, but she had her first real premonition a few weeks ago," Missy said with a wistful smile. "She was at a bank and picked up the pen at the counter after a woman with two small children had used it. She said the woman had felt happy and at peace when she used the pen, but then Clarissa saw a vision of the woman being hit by a car after she walked out of the bank. Clarissa wasn't even sure if it was true or if she was crazy, but she stopped the woman and delayed her by asking about her children's school.

A few moments later a car careened out of control and hit a pole right outside the bank. It was just as Clarissa had seen in her vision, except that the woman wasn't harmed."

"That's amazing," Piper said, her thoughts turning to Phoebe and her power of premonition. She was happy to hear that Clarissa used her premonitions to help people as well. Sometimes people with power like that didn't know how to control it and ended up using it for their own gain. Or for simple, good old, run-of-the-mill evil.

"No one else in our coven even approaches that kind of gift," Missy said.

Maybe someone didn't want her to use it on him, Piper thought, a little line of sweat popping up along her forehead. *Maybe someone wanted to silence her power.* She felt her heart start to pound, and suddenly she needed to get out of there and find her sisters. She had to make sure they were okay.

"How many people know about Clarissa's power?" Piper asked, wiping her hands on the thighs of her jeans.

"Just the coven," Missy replied. "You can imagine why she wouldn't want it advertised. If the wrong people found out . . ."

Missy trailed off, and she and Piper exchanged a look. They both knew exactly what could happen if the wrong people found out. It already had.

"Well, thank you for your time," Piper said, rising from the couch.

"Do you think there's any chance they'll find her?" Missy asked, practically jumping out of her seat to follow Piper to the door.

"We're going to do everything we can, I promise," Piper said comfortingly. "Someone will be in touch."

She turned and headed for the SUV, her pace quickening with each step. All she wanted to do was find Daryl, Paige, and Phoebe and tell them the news—she had a possible motive. And if she was right, the Charmed Ones were definitely in danger.

"This house is huge," Paige said to Elijah Baker as he led her through one living room and into another. Her high-heeled boots clicked loudly on the freshly buffed marble floor. "Your mortgage must be pretty steep."

Elijah was a member of a coven of male and female Wiccans that had lost one of their members the week before. His home was an old, classic Victorian but was decorated with modern styles—a lot of black leather and chrome. It was the kind of place that made Paige too intimidated to touch anything and made her pull her leather jacket closer to her body so that she wouldn't bump into anything, either. It was beautiful, but not exactly welcoming.

"Well, I don't live here alone," Elijah said as

he stepped over to a huge slate fireplace. He took down a large photograph of about a dozen people set inside a shining silver frame. "Most of the members of the coven live here as well. Kind of a . . . mystical frat house, if you will. Except that some of the women live here, too."

"Oh, well, that's cool," Paige said, feeling completely inarticulate. Normally Paige could talk to anyone, but something about Elijah and about her surroundings was throwing her.

He handed her the photograph and Paige looked it over, a slight shiver running over her skin. All the men and women in the picture looked so stern and rigid. Not a single one of them was smiling. Apparently these people took their coven very seriously.

"That's Samson in the center," Elijah said, crossing his arms over his chest.

Paige looked at the missing Wiccan and found herself suddenly smiling. Samson was a well-built, handsome African-American man with a shaved head and light brown eyes. Even though his mouth was set in a straight line like everyone else's, she could tell his eyes were smiling. She knew on instinct that Samson was a nice person—someone who could kick back and relax even in the midst of all the proper people that seemed to surround him.

Suddenly Elijah slipped the frame from her hands and replaced it carefully on the mantel, adjusting it until it was perfectly straight and centered.

"Let's go to the kitchen," he said, turning quickly on his heel.

Paige flushed at his clipped and cold tone, wondering if she had done something to offend him. Elijah was plain, tall, and lanky with light brown hair and brown eyes, and his manner was detached and almost off-putting. Not what she would have expected from a Wiccan. She always pictured other witches as spiritual, all-loving, patient, and kind. Of course, that snap assessment was just as judgmental as Piper's idea that all Wiccans were touchy-feely wanna-bes. Besides, she had to cut the guy some slack. He had just lost one of his friends.

Paige followed him into the next room, where he sat down at the head of a long chrome kitchen table with eight black high-backed chairs around it. She lowered herself into the chair catty-corner from Elijah's. It was hard as a rock, so she sat forward slightly in an attempt to get comfortable. She looked at Elijah, and he gazed back at her with narrowed eyes, as if he was sizing her up.

"Does Samson live here?" Paige asked, trying to straighten her posture and appear official under Elijah's watchful gaze. She always hated posing as someone who worked with the police department—the part of a stuffed shirt just didn't suit her.

"Yes. He was kidnapped from here," Elijah answered. He settled his elbows on the armrests of his chair and folded his hands away from his chest. Paige saw the muscles in his jaw working as if he was angry or thinking of something he didn't like to remember.

"Are you all right?" Paige asked.

"I'm fine," Elijah answered, his eyes flicking over her. "It's just that he was sleeping right down the hall from me and a half dozen of our brethren. I don't understand how we didn't hear anything. I suppose these people knew what they were doing."

Paige's heart went out to Elijah. Cold-mannered or not, he was clearly hurting. "It's not your fault," she told him, resisting the urge to touch his arm. She had a feeling Elijah was not the type that liked to be touched by strangers.

He took in a long, deep breath and stared toward the large glass bowl that sat empty at the center of the table. There were a few moments of tension-filled silence, and Paige actually thought of getting up to leave. This guy was not a talker. But she'd barely found out a thing—certainly nothing interesting to tell Daryl and her sisters. So she simply sat and waited, hoping Elijah would choose to say more.

"I don't know what we're going to do without him," Elijah said finally, so quietly that Paige wasn't certain she'd heard him right.

"You miss him, huh?" she asked, shifting in her seat. Her vinyl pants made a loud squeaking sound against the hard seat, and she blushed. "Sorry."

"It's okay," Elijah said. "Happens all the time." He actually shot her a tight smile, and Paige felt her shoulder muscles uncurl. "Yes, I miss Samson. He's like a brother to me. But it's not just that," Elijah said.

He paused, and Paige sensed he was going to need a little push to keep going. "What is it?" she asked gently. "Was he your high priest?"

She felt a little surge of pride at simply knowing this terminology. At least her hour of surfing the Wicca Web sites had proved useful in *some* capacity.

"He was," Elijah answered, leaning his weight into his left arm. "Or *is*," he corrected himself, clearing his throat. Clearly he was not ready to think of Samson in the past tense. "He inspires everyone. He has this power. . . ." He glanced up at Paige as if to see how she would react to the word *power*, but Paige simply gazed back at him, her brown eyes steady. "He's able to see auras quite clearly, and he was honing the ability to cleanse. He did a cleansing on me after my mother passed away, and it was incredibly helpful. It helped me to put the past behind me and move ahead. . . ."

Elijah trailed off and clenched his jaw,

obviously uncomfortable with the personal turn he'd allowed himself to take in the conversation. He let out a sigh—a short burst of frustrated breath—and looked at Paige once more.

"Does anyone else in your coven have this power?" Paige asked gently.

"No," Elijah said. "We have power together, of course, but Samson is the gifted one in our circle. He's helped a lot of people."

"He sounds like a good guy," Paige said, realizing her words probably sounded trite to Elijah, but feeling the need to say something.

"Please find him," Elijah said firmly. "I honestly don't know what we'll do here without him."

Paige swallowed hard and pushed her chair back from the table, sensing she'd just been given the cue to go. "We'll try," she said with a small smile. "Thank you for your time."

"I'll walk you to the door," Elijah said, starting to rise.

"No, please," Paige said, holding out her hand. "I'm fine."

She turned and walked out to the front living room, then checked over her shoulder. She'd lent Phoebe her car, and Piper had the SUV, so she'd orbed herself onto Elijah's street and she was going to have to orb herself back to the manor. At that moment she was glad to have the lightning-speed mode of transport. Seeing Elijah so broken up about Samson had left her with a sickening urge to see her sisters. She couldn't imagine what she would do if her own "coven" suffered a loss like Elijah's. Paige closed her eyes and orbed herself back to her home.

"All right, let me get this straight," Phoebe said, standing in the middle of the living room at Halliwell Manor, one shaky hand to her forehead. Piper was leaning against the mantel to her right, and Daryl and Paige were seated on the couch, looking up at her expectantly. "Both Samson and Clarissa were the most powerful Wiccans in their covens? They both had actual powers?"

"Looks that way," Paige said, folding her hands over one knee and leaning back into the couch.

"Well, that's disturbing," Phoebe said, rubbing her forehead for good measure before dropping her hand again. "Keisha was the high priestess of her coven, too. Apparently she had the power to see through solid objects."

"A Superwoman Wiccan?" Piper asked without a trace of irony.

"Something like that," Phoebe answered. She walked behind her favorite chair and leaned against the back. Her heart was in her throat and pounding hard. The pieces of the puzzle were starting to fit together, and she didn't like the picture that was forming before her.

"Someone's trying to silence a lot of power," Piper said, pushing her hand into her hair and resting her elbow on the mantel. She held her hair back from her face and stared at the picture frames in front of her.

"Or trying to *gather* a lot of power," Phoebe said.

Piper's head popped up and Paige sat forward. Phoebe could tell from their expressions that this was something neither of them had considered, but it was perfectly clear to her. If the other Wiccans that had been kidnapped were each as gifted as the three they'd learned about today, then someone was compiling an arsenal of mystical power. Who knew what the kidnapper wanted to use these Wiccans for.

"Wait a minute," Daryl said, sliding forward on the couch. "Are you saying that someone could be trying to put together an army?"

"Something like that," Phoebe said. "But it could be worse. These Wiccans all seem like good people, so it wouldn't be easy to turn them evil, but if we're dealing with a warlock . . ."

Phoebe paused and looked at Piper, holding her breath.

"Warlocks . . . right. Remind me," Daryl demanded, looking from Phoebe to Piper and back again. "What's the deal with warlocks?"

"When a warlock kills a real witch, he absorbs his or her power and is able to use it,"

Phoebe explained, standing up straight and pushing her hands into the back pockets of her slacks. "If we're dealing with a warlock or some other power-sucking demon—"

"Then one guy could have all of these powers by now," Paige said, her voice filled with fear.

"And my guess is he's not planning on using them to do good," Piper put in as she stepped away from the wall.

"Okay, I *really* don't like this," Daryl said, pushing his hands into his thighs and standing up. "I think you guys need to get out of here . . . now."

"Daryl, what are you talking about?" Paige asked, scrunching up her face.

"I'm talking about getting you to a safe house or something," Daryl replied earnestly. "If these people are rounding up powerful witches, it's only a matter of time before they show up at your door."

"They're taking only the *most* powerful of each coven," Paige pointed out. "I wonder who they'd take from the three of us," she said, glancing at Phoebe, her eyebrows raised.

"I'd have to go with Piper," Phoebe said with a thoughtful frown.

"Please!" Piper replied, shaking her head. "Phoebe's the number one badass around here. You can freakin' fly!"

"But don't discount Paige," Phoebe put in,

lifting her index finger. "She's pretty wily with all that disappearing stuff."

"Thank you!" Paige said, throwing up her hands. "I was starting to feel like chopped liver over here."

"Ladies!" Daryl exclaimed, frustrated.

Phoebe and her sisters laughed, but when Daryl shot her his best *I mean business* cop stare, Phoebe covered her mouth and made herself get serious. "Sorry," she said. "Just a little comic relief."

"Well, I'm not in the mood," Daryl said. "I'm surprised these people, or things, or warlocks, or whatever, haven't already come after you three."

"Well, we're not gonna run. We never have before, and we're not going to start now," Piper said, walking around the couch and sitting down next to Paige. She slipped her arm over Paige's shoulders and looked up at Daryl. "We know how to take care of ourselves. We're just going to have to keep our eyes peeled."

"Exactly," Phoebe said, feeling wary and determined at the same time. "The question is . . . for what?"

Chapter
3

Paige pulled her favorite baggy sweatshirt out of her dresser and slipped it on over her head, sighing contentedly as the fuzzy material settled in around her skin. After a day like this all she could think about was changing into her comfy clothes. If some wacko was going to come grab her out of her own house, she may as well be comfortable for the occasion. Besides, it would be best to have the benefit of unhindered movement, just in case she needed to kick a little butt.

Downstairs Daryl, Piper, and Phoebe were still talking, and the sound of their muffled voices coming up through the floorboards was comforting to Paige as well. Having her family near her filled her with a sensation of warmth and serenity. Like there was nothing she couldn't handle. She and her sisters had been through a lot together and had always come out okay. As long as they were here for her, she knew nothing bad could happen.

Well, maybe something *bad* could happen, but it wouldn't be the end of the world. Most likely.

Paige turned and was about to head back downstairs when something caught her attention out of the corner of her eye—a tightly crumpled ball of paper lying in the bottom of her trash can. Suddenly Paige's face lit up. An idea was rapidly forming in her head. No, not just an idea, but a plan! She grabbed the ball of paper and flew out of her room, nearly trembling with excitement.

Here I come to save the day! Paige thought as she skipped down the stairs and into the kitchen, where the others had moved their conversation.

"You guys, you guys, you guys! I figured it out!" Paige said, sliding across the room in her socked feet. Piper, Phoebe, and Daryl were sitting around the kitchen table, and Daryl moved his chair aside when it became clear that Paige was going to barrel right into his back if he didn't.

"Figured what out?" Piper asked, her forehead crinkling as Paige uncrumpled the paper.

"How to find out who's doing the kidnappings," Paige said, flushed with triumph. "Or *what*, that is."

"Okay, I don't understand why you're showing this to me again," Phoebe said, looking at the computer printout.

"We have to go to the Gathering!" Paige exclaimed, tossing the paper onto the table in front of them.

"Not this again," Piper said, slumping back in her chair.

"What's a Gathering?" Daryl asked. He glanced warily at the paper, clearly taking his cue from Piper's and Phoebe's less than enthused expressions.

"It's a Gathering of the Covens!" Paige exclaimed, undeterred. This time she knew she was right, and there was no way they could say no to her plan. "Wiccans from across the country are going to be getting together in Las Vegas next week!"

"And?" Daryl prompted.

Phoebe sat up straight, realization dawning on her face. "And if this kidnapper wants more Wiccans . . ."

"And if he has any brains . . . ," Piper put in slowly.

"Then he's definitely going to be there!" Paige said triumphantly, crossing her arms over her chest. She watched Phoebe and Piper exchange a glance, and she knew she had them. Ha! For once the little sister had come up with the master plan! "Why bother traveling all over the place looking for Wiccans when you can go to Vegas and have a Wiccan buffet?!"

Phoebe tilted her head to one side and pressed her lips together, impressed. "The girl is good."

"We've taught her well," Piper deadpanned.

"What am I missing here?" Daryl asked. "You're not telling me you want to go to this thing."

"Using the term 'want' very loosely," Piper said through her teeth, flinging her long hair over her shoulder and drawing the wrinkled paper toward her.

"Wait a minute, wait a minute," Daryl said. He thrust his arms out over the table. "This is where I draw the line. I agree with you. I think the kidnapper would be an idiot not to look for his next victim at this Gathering thing. But that's exactly why you should stay as far away from there as possible."

Paige scoffed and pulled her hands up into the sleeves of her sweatshirt. "Daryl, come on," she said, leaning back against the center island.

"I'm serious, Paige," he said, turning around fully in his seat so he could see her. "Why set yourselves up to be kidnapped?"

"What else are we going to do?" Phoebe asked. "Sit around here and wait for this guy to come get us? That's not my idea of a plan."

Paige grinned at her sister. *My thoughts exactly.* The Charmed Ones were not in the habit of being sitting ducks. There was something seriously evil out there, and they had the perfect opportunity to find it before it did any more harm. They couldn't just ignore that. They had to be on the offensive, not the defensive.

"Paige and Phoebe are right," Piper said, folding the piece of paper with the Gathering info as neatly as possible, considering how destroyed it was. She stood up and leaned over the table to hand it back to Paige. "I say we lure this thing out and deal with it. Get this over and done with. Paige, you make the reservations. I have to make some calls and see who can cover for me at P3."

Phoebe slapped her palms on the table and pushed herself up. "And I'm going to have to have a nice long argument with my boss," she said.

Daryl let out a deep sigh and tucked his chin toward his chest, but said nothing more. The poor guy knew when he was outnumbered and outpowered. The moment Paige realized he was resigned to the inevitable, she raised her fists in the air in triumph. *Gathering of the Covens, here we come!*

"We're going to Vegas, baby!"

• • •

Piper stood in front of her closet and gazed at the racks of clothing, paralyzed. There was an open suitcase on the bed behind her that was completely empty except for a few pairs of underwear. Aside from the problem of packing for a trip that she didn't exactly want to go on was the problem of packing for Las Vegas in the middle of June.

"I don't own enough tank tops," Piper said to herself.

She walked into the closet gamely and turned on the light, then yanked a few tops down from their hangers arbitrarily. It wasn't like she was going to be trying to impress anybody on this trip. Who cared what she wore? When she walked out again, Leo was standing right in the middle of their room. Piper dropped her shirts, and her hands flew up reflexively at the sight of a surprise visitor, but she stopped herself from using her power just in time. Meanwhile, Leo hit the floor.

"Don't *do* that," Piper said, her whole body tense. "I almost blew you into tiny little Leo pieces."

"Sorry," Leo said, pushing himself up and dusting off the front of his blue plaid shirt. "I'll try to orb more loudly next time."

"Thank you," she said. She bent to pick up her shirts, which had scattered on the floor, and tossed them into her suitcase. She couldn't remember the last time she was so unpsyched to pack for a trip. Just the sight of the suitcase depressed her.

"I can't help but notice you're packing," Leo said, eyeing the tangled mess of clothes on their bed.

"Yeah, we're going to Las Vegas," Piper said, not even trying to hide her disdain as she pulled open her sock drawer. "What do you think it is there this time of year, like eight *billion* degrees?"

"That's a bit of an exaggeration," Leo said. "It's probably more like seven billion."

Piper snorted a laugh, gathered up a slew of socks in her arms, and stalked over to the bed, where she dumped them into the suitcase. As she was heading back for the closet Leo caught her up in his arms and held her from behind.

"Okay, stop moving. You're making me tense," he said, resting his chin on her shoulder. "Why don't you tell me what's going on?"

Just the feel of his arms around her made Piper calm down the slightest bit. She pulled away from his grasp and turned so she could face him, resting her palms on his chest.

"Paige found out about this Coven Gathering in Las Vegas for the summer solstice, and we figure if this kidnapper wants some more

Wiccans, he's going to be there," she explained, picking a piece of lint off his shirt.

"So you're gonna go find him and save the day," Leo said with a thoughtful frown. "Good plan. I don't like that it puts you directly in the line of fire, but it's a good plan."

"I know," Piper said, moving away from him and sitting down on the edge of their mattress. "I just really didn't want to go to this thing." She lifted her shoulders in a *What can I do?* gesture and glanced up at him. "What did the Elders have to say?"

"Not much, unfortunately," Leo replied, sitting down next to her. He laced his fingers through hers and pulled her hand toward him. "They're concerned, obviously, but as far as they can tell, no dangerously powerful demons have escaped the underworld recently, so—"

"But it has to be a demon," Piper said. "Or if not, a warlock. We figured out that the Wiccans being kidnapped are majorly powerful. Phoebe thinks someone's trying to put together some big mystical wattage."

"So a warlock makes sense," Leo said, narrowing his eyes. "When I go back up, I'll have to suggest that to them."

"But not yet, right?" Piper said, squeezing his hand. "You're not going back up yet."

Leo smiled and slipped his strong arms around her, holding her tightly. "Nah. I think I'll hang here with you for a while," Leo responded, leaning over to plant a kiss on her forehead. "You know, help you pack for a trip you don't want to go on."

"Thanks," Piper said with a sigh and a smile. She got up and headed into her closet again. She paused near the shelves in the back, looking wistfully at her bathing suits and wishing for a split second that she was, in fact, packing for a trip to the islands with Leo instead of for this crazy mission. But her Charmed destiny came first. She shook her head to clear the daydream and grabbed an armful of chinos and jeans. This time when she emerged from the closet, Cole and Phoebe were standing in the middle of the room.

"All right, that's it. I'm putting bells on you people," Piper said sarcastically, dropping her clothes onto the bed.

"Sorry," Phoebe said with an apologetic smile. "We were just thinking we should probably bring some protection crystals or something, just in case."

"I don't like the idea of you three going in there with nothing at your back," Cole added firmly.

Piper glanced at her future brother-in-law, thinking not for the first time that there was a reason he was such a good lawyer. When a guy that big, that broad, that brooding, dark, and serious, said something, you pretty much believed it. He was wearing a pair of gray suit pants and a dark blue shirt with the sleeves rolled up. His near-black hair was still gelled back after a day of interviews, and it was clear from his disturbed expression that Phoebe had just filled him in on the events of the day.

"I don't know if we need to bother, you guys," Piper said, folding a pair of chinos over her arm. "I mean, it's not like we can't handle ourselves with a demon or a warlock. I think it's all the witch wanna-bes we should really be concerned about."

Piper suddenly had a mental picture of a bunch of Missy Stark-like hippies dancing naked around a bonfire. It wasn't a pretty sight, and she hoped her imagination was *very* far from the truth. She wasn't going to be taking her clothes off for anything. Especially if a warlock might strike at any second. Now *that* would give the underworld something to gossip about.

"They have a point, honey," Leo said, jarring Piper out of her silly stream of thoughts. "Better safe than sorry, right?"

"We can call you if we need you," Piper told him, adding her chinos to the mess of clothing in her bag. "Don't worry about it."

"Piper, I don't understand," Phoebe said, an edge creeping into her voice. "Sixteen witches have disappeared without a trace. How can you be so casual about this?"

"They are Wiccans, not witches," Piper corrected almost sternly. "And I'm not being casual about it. I'm just being . . . confident." She dropped a pair of shorts into her bag and tossed her hair over her shoulder nonchalantly. "I know that whatever this thing is, we're going to be able to deal with it."

"I'm glad you're so sure of yourself, Piper, but from what Phoebe tells me, these people aren't just run-of-the-mill Wiccans," Cole interjected hotly. "If they have the powers their friends say they do, then they are witches *and* Wiccans, and they couldn't protect themselves."

"Cole, calm down," Piper said, spreading her fingers out in front of her. "Everything is going to be fine. No one is going to get hurt."

She spun toward her closet again, figuring the conversation was over, but no one else moved. Piper felt a little sliver of tension curl its way through her spine, and she turned slowly to look at them.

"At least, no one is going to get hurt if you all leave me alone and let me pack," she said through her teeth.

"Fine," Phoebe said, rolling her eyes. She and Cole swept out of the room, leaving Piper and Leo alone once again.

"You okay?" Leo asked, concerned.

"I'm great," Piper said. "I just think all this talk of vacations has made me realize that I need one."

"Well, you're *kind of* getting one," Leo suggested helpfully.

Piper simply grunted as she slapped closed her half-packed bag. "Yeah," she said sarcastically. "I wish."

Chapter
4

"Can you believe this place?" Phoebe asked, her eyes wide open in wonder as Paige drove her two sisters down the Strip in Las Vegas. It was pitch black out, but the bright lights of the Strip were almost blinding. Paige could see everything around her in stark detail. It was almost brighter than daylight.

"No, not really," Piper replied from the backseat of the sweet convertible the sisters had rented at the Las Vegas airport. She pulled her cardigan on as a breeze lifted her hair from her neck. There was a slight chill in the air that none of them had expected. Apparently the desert nights weren't quite as hot as the desert days. "I mean, we've seen some strange things in our day . . . ," Piper continued, staring out the side of the car.

She eyed a couple of showgirls who were walking down the sidewalk in gold lamé bikinis with long turquoise feathers rising out of their headpieces. They had on four-inch heels and towered over the man who walked between them, chewing on a cigar and stuffing a thick money clip back into his suit pocket. A couple of girls dressed up as Dorothy from *The Wizard of Oz* strolled by smoking cigarettes, and a pack of guys in Hawaiian shirts stopped them to try out their pick-up lines.

"I think it's cool," Paige protested, leaning her arm on the top of her door and taking a nice deep breath of the fresh, dry air.

It was a perfect, clear night, and the tourists were out in droves, walking in groups from one casino to another, holding little plastic cups of their winnings. People kept stopping and pointing out various sights to their friends—the huge pirate ship in front of Treasure Island, the monstrous columns surrounding Caesars. Each casino was more elaborate than the last. Paige had seen pictures and movies of this place all her life, but none of them had done the city justice.

For one, Las Vegas was immaculately clean. There wasn't a piece of stray garbage in sight. No graffiti. It was like someone had just come through and steam-cleaned the whole place. And the lights, while admittedly way, *way* over the top, were actually kind of beautiful. In a spectacular kind of way.

"Oooh! Look at that!" Phoebe exclaimed, grabbing Paige's arm. "All-you-can-eat breakfast buffet! A dollar ninety-nine!"

"You're kidding," Paige said, taking her eyes off the road long enough to check out the huge neon sign. Then she saw another: ALL-YOU-CAN-EAT SURF 'N' TURF! $2.99! And another: NON-STOP EATS! $1.99! Paige started to salivate right there behind the wheel. The tiny little meal they'd been given on the plane hadn't exactly done it for her.

"We may need to buy ourselves some bigger clothes while we're here," Piper said wryly.

Paige and Phoebe laughed as Paige pulled to a stop at a red light right in between four of the biggest casinos on the Strip. The MGM Grand was ahead to the left—huge and green and shimmering like its own Emerald City. To the right was the Excalibur, which was definitely Paige's favorite. It was a big white castle with colorful turrets and a wizard—Merlin most likely—looking down from one of the highest windows. Maybe it was Paige's old obsession with fairy tales, but she really wished they were staying at the Excalibur.

"Paige, I have to say, getting a convertible was an inspired idea," Piper said, leaning back and stretching her arms out across the backseat. She tipped her face toward the sky. "I haven't been this relaxed in weeks, even if there is a witch-kidnapping fiend on the loose."

"I'm glad, Piper," Paige said, glancing in the rearview mirror with a smile. She bit her tongue to keep from letting out an "I told you so." Instead, she said a silent thank-you to the powers that be that her sisters finally seemed to be getting into the spirit of things. Especially Piper. She'd been so grumpy before they left, Paige was starting to rethink the intelligence of her plan. She had visions of herself listening to nothing but biting remarks from Piper for the next few days and briefly considered orbing to Alaska and forgetting the whole thing.

"You guys! Check it out!" Phoebe exclaimed as Paige hit the gas again. They were passing by the mini skyline that made up the New York, New York casino. A replica of the Brooklyn Bridge served as an elevated sidewalk, and there was even a mini Statue of Liberty and an Empire State Building. A roller coaster came roaring by, making its way around the outside of the casino, its passengers screaming and laughing. "That's it. I'm moving here," Phoebe added. "I had no idea this place was going to be so cool!"

"I wonder which casino we're staying in," Piper said, pulling the Gathering of the Covens info sheet out of her inside jacket pocket. "It says 'four-star accommodations.' Do you think they'll have a masseuse?"

"Probably," Paige said gleefully, glancing down at the directions in her lap. "Maybe we'll even have a Jacuzzi in our room!"

"I'm tellin' ya," Phoebe said, flipping the visor down. "These Wiccan people really know how to do it up."

She pulled a lipstick out of her purse and started to fix her makeup as Paige turned down a side street, leaving the main strip behind. Paige glanced at her directions again, making sure she'd gotten it right. All the biggest casinos were on the Strip, right? So where, exactly, were these directions taking her? Glancing in the rearview mirror again, she saw that Piper was resting with her eyes closed once more. That was probably a good thing. If Piper saw where they were going, she'd probably start getting all worked up.

And for no reason, Paige told herself, making another turn. *There has to be some huge hotel back here, or another casino that's just off the Strip. It says "four-star accommodations."*

"Hey, it's really dark," Phoebe said, looking away from the visor mirror for a moment. Little concerned lines formed at the top of her nose as she looked around. "Paige, where are we going? Where's the city?"

"Uh . . . I don't know," Paige said uncertainly. "I'm just following the directions."

"Are you sure?" Piper asked. Suddenly her face was right between Paige's and Phoebe's as she leaned in from the backseat. "There's nothing out here."

Paige bit her bottom lip and tried not to get too worried. But Piper was right. They were definitely outside the city limits now, and there weren't even that many streetlamps to light the way. What kind of four-star hotel was out in the middle of the desert?

"I don't like this," Phoebe said, glancing back toward the glowing city. "This feels wrong."

"Maybe we should turn around," Piper said. "You know . . . start over."

"You guys, I know how to follow directions," Paige said, her face heating up slightly.

"Well, you must have done *something* wrong," Piper said. "We're in the middle of nowhere."

As irritated as she was, Paige was about to admit that her sisters could be right and turn the car around, when she saw the shadow of something on the side of the road up ahead.

"Wait!" Paige exclaimed. "I think I see a sign up there! Yeah. I think this is where we make our last turn."

Paige rolled the car to a stop next to the large sign, which stood at the end of a dirt road. It wasn't very well lit, so Paige turned on the car's brights so that she and her sisters could read. The moment she saw the words painted on the rickety wooden sign, her stomach turned and she swallowed hard, dreading the total melt-down that was about to take place.

"'Welcome to Tumbleweed Campground,'" Phoebe read slowly, as if she couldn't herself believe what she was saying. "'Las Vegas's only *four-star* camping facility.'"

There was a smallish piece of paper tacked to the bottom of the sign, flapping in the breeze, that read WELCOME TO THE GATHERING OF THE COVENS! Whoever had written it had run out of room and had to squeeze in the word *covens* by making the letters progressively smaller and smaller. Definitely not a sign of a well-organized event.

"We're staying on a *campground*?" Piper asked incredulously.

Paige turned to look at her sisters, trying to ignore the daggers shooting out of their eyes. Suddenly she was glad that neither of them had the power of deadly sight.

"Well . . . it makes sense when you think about it," she said with a hopeful smile. "You know, part of being a Wiccan is communing with nature, and . . . honestly, I think that's something that we don't do enough of."

"Nice cover, Paige," Phoebe said, slumping back in her seat. "You better just hope they have toilets in this place, or I am calling Leo to orb me straight home."

"So much for the masseuse," Piper said. She sat back in her seat again, and Paige put the car into gear and started down the long, winding dirt road toward the campground. For the next few minutes not a word was said between them. Apparently the positive-thinking portion of this vacation was officially over.

Phoebe pulled her rolling suitcase along the bumpy dirt path behind Piper, Paige, and Marcia Farina, the coordinator of the Gathering of the Covens. Every time the bag hit a rock, it tipped over and Phoebe had to stop, turn around, and struggle to right it again. As they passed by large khaki tents and little groups of Wiccans, Phoebe tried to smile politely, but she couldn't help feeling entirely out of place. Which was interesting, considering she and her sisters may very well have been the only true witches there. She just wished she had been forewarned that this was going to be a camping trip. She would have worn cargo pants and sneakers instead of a colorful ankle-length skirt and heeled sandals. And she definitely would have brought a backpack.

"I'm so glad you girls could make it!" Marcia said with a high-wattage smile that seemed more than a little bit forced. Her short black hair was blowing all over the place in the desert wind, but she didn't seem to notice. She clutched a clipboard in front of her shimmery purple shirt and practically skipped as she led them along. For a middle-aged woman, Marcia was kind of hyper. Normally Phoebe would think her energy was sweet and inspiring, but this energy seemed to stem from nervousness. Marcia was definitely a little wound about something. "So many covens canceled this year, I wasn't even sure we were going to be able to have the event."

"Why did they cancel?" Phoebe asked, even though she was pretty sure she knew the answer. She yanked her bag over a lump in the path and hoped they were close to whatever tent they were going to be calling home for the next few days.

"Oh . . . the kidnappings," Marcia said with a wave of her hand, as if she just didn't want to think about it. "They thought the Gathering would be a prime attraction for whoever is doing this. You have heard about the kidnappings, haven't you?"

"We have," Piper said calmly, tucking her hair behind her ear and adjusting the strap of her own heavy bag.

"And you're not concerned?" Marcia asked.

Phoebe looked at her sisters before choosing her words carefully. "Well . . . we can take care of ourselves," she said finally.

Marcia laughed. "That's the spirit. I'm glad you girls aren't intimidated. If you let yourselves be intimidated, then the bad guys have already won, am I right?"

She stopped and looked at them for approval, and Phoebe simply smiled. "Exactly," she said.

"Now, this is the dining hall," Marcia explained, quickly changing gears. She pointed behind her to a long, low cabin. "Mealtimes are marked on the itineraries I gave you when you arrived."

Thank heaven for that, Phoebe thought, glad to know she wasn't going to have to be cooking her own food over an open flame.

"Let's keep moving," Marcia said.

She was off again like a shot, and Phoebe yanked on her suitcase behind her. Marcia pointed out a few bathroom cabins as well, and Phoebe started to relax a bit. Maybe this wouldn't be so bad after all. It wasn't a big, flashy casino, but at least there was some version of indoor plumbing.

"Well, here we are! Tent number thirty-two!" Marcia trilled, stopping in front of a large army-green tent. It had a solid wooden frame, and the cloth covering was securely tied to the ground all around the perimeter. It looked sturdy enough.

Phoebe looked at Piper and Paige. "Well, go ahead in," she said.

"I think Paige should go first," Piper said with a sardonic smile.

"I think I will!" Paige said brightly.

She thrust aside the door flap and stepped inside. Phoebe heard some fumbling and a muffled "Ow!" but a moment later a light emanated from within the tent. Phoebe and Piper exchanged a look. Light was good.

"Hey! This is pretty nice!" Paige called out, sounding genuinely impressed.

Phoebe walked inside and was surprised to find that the tent was very spacious and clean. The floor was made of solid, packed dirt, and one cot stood against each of the three full walls, covered with pillows and bright white sheets. Paige had lit a lantern that stood on a small table against the back of the tent, and there were two more lanterns in the corners. Phoebe walked over to the nearest cot and hoisted her bag up onto it. It creaked loudly and sagged in the middle, but that was to be expected. Phoebe had packed for a whirlwind casino vacation *and* for some demon butt-kicking. It was hard to down-size with two such different missions in mind.

"Well, thanks again for coming," Marcia said, holding the door flap up. "If you have any questions, you can see either myself or Ryan Treetop. He's the owner of the campground, and I share his office while I'm here. I'll see you at the meet-and-greet tonight." She started to step out, but paused and popped her head back into the tent. "Oh! And don't forget, you'll need to let me know if you want anything special said at the rededication ceremony."

Phoebe looked at her sisters, but they both appeared as clueless as she was. Even Paige's face was blank.

"Rededication ceremony?" Piper asked.

Marcia stopped once again and looked at them, confused. Paige pressed her eyes closed in embarrassment, and Phoebe realized that anyone who showed up at this Gathering was probably supposed to know what a rededication ceremony was.

"Um . . . what do you mean, 'anything special'?" Phoebe asked.

Marcia came all the way back into the tent and stood up straight, holding her clipboard against her chest. "I'm sorry, I thought you were aware of the tradition," she said, making Phoebe feel like a kid who had just given the wrong answer in class. "Each year at the Gathering all the covens come together on the night of the summer solstice and rededicate themselves to the Wiccan craft and to the Goddess and the Horned God."

Piper let out a little snort, and Phoebe and Paige both leveled her with a glare. The last thing Phoebe wanted was for this woman to think they were laughing at her. They had to blend in as a coven that was actually *into* this stuff. Covering quickly, Piper started to cough and turned her back on Marcia, searching through her bag and coming out with a water bottle.

"Sorry," she said after taking a long drink of water. "The dry air gets to me."

Marcia looked unconvinced, but she was apparently willing to let it slide. "As I was saying, each coven usually submits a passage to be read at the ceremony," she said, directing her comments to Phoebe. "It makes it more personal."

"I see," Phoebe said with a smile. She could tell Piper was struggling to keep from cracking up laughing, so she reached out and grabbed her sister's wrist in an attempt to ground her. "I'll write something up as soon as I can."

"Thank you," Marcia said with a smile. Then she shot Piper a reproving look and disappeared through the door.

The moment Phoebe released her grip on Piper, she burst out laughing. "I think I just got on Marcia's bad side," she said, lowering herself onto her cot.

"Well, that was kind of rude, Piper," Paige said, putting her hands on her hips.

"You don't even talk to me," Piper said, only semiseriously. "I mean, the *Horned God*? Paige, what have you gotten us into?"

Paige simply shrugged and screwed her face up apologetically. "I've been doing some reading, but I guess I haven't gotten as far as the Horned God," she said.

"Hey, let's remember we're here for a reason," Phoebe said. "We might not be in the middle of the Vegas action, but maybe that's a good thing. No distractions means we can concentrate on finding the kidnapper."

"Good point," Piper said.

"Thank you," Phoebe said, unzipping her suitcase. "Now, let's get dressed and go to this meet-and-greet thing and see what we can find out."

Chapter
5

"Everybody ready?" Phoebe asked, pulling her long hot-pink sweater on over her tank top. Piper wrapped her hair into a ponytail and snapped the rubber band, and Paige pulled on a pair of sneakers, stifling a huge yawn.

"I'm exhausted from that flight. Who has a meet-and-greet at midnight, anyway?" Paige asked, stretching her arms above her head.

"Hey, you're the one who wanted to learn more about Wicca," Piper said as she headed for the door. "Take a note, they're night people."

"Ha, ha," Paige said with a smirk. She slipped through the door as Piper held the flap aside, and Phoebe followed.

"How do we know where we're . . ."

Phoebe's question died in her throat the moment she hit the fresh air. Dozens of people were streaming out of tents toward an incredibly bright light in the center of the camp area. Smoke and embers rose into the night sky, and even from this distance Phoebe could hear the crackling of a huge fire. The sweet, musky smell of burning wood filled the air.

"Never mind," she said.

Piper led the way along the path that wound between the tents. As they walked Phoebe studied some of the other Wiccans, all of whom seemed to be staying with their own covens. It was bizarre how easily she could tell who was with whom. There was a group of women who were all dressed in gauzy white gowns and had adorned their hair with flowers. Following behind them was a rowdy bunch of hippie types, all of whom wore cutoff cargo pants or jeans and were chanting something that had to do with the moon and stars.

Phoebe and her sisters had a familial resemblance, but they didn't exactly travel in uniform. Piper was wearing a sensible V-necked top and jeans, Paige had on a pair of trendy silver nylon track pants and a bright red T-shirt, and Phoebe was wearing a belly-bearing tank top under her cardigan, along with a pair of brightly flowered capri pants.

"Maybe we should have come up with some kind of outfit," Phoebe said out of the side of her mouth.

"Yeah. Printed T-shirts that say 'The Charmed Ones' in big neon letters," Piper replied with a laugh.

Just as Phoebe and her sisters were about to reach the bonfire, a huge group of young women, all dressed head-to-toe in black, streamed out of a pathway to the right, cutting them off. Each one looked a little bit more irritated than the last.

"They didn't even give us a place to hang our clothes," a girl with purple hair and very black eyeliner muttered.

Paige rolled her eyes, but Phoebe looked away so that her sister couldn't read her face. That was her one and only complaint about the tent as well.

Once all the Goth girls had filed past, Piper walked to the opening between the last two tents and paused. Paige and Phoebe came up behind her, and Phoebe stood up on her tiptoes to see over her sister's shoulder. Her mouth instantly dropped open in awe. The fire was even bigger than she had expected. Huge, tree-trunk-size logs were gathered together in a monstrous pyramid, and flames shot so high into the air it almost seemed like a volcano. The heat coming from the center of the clearing was intense.

"Look at all these people," Paige said, gazing at the groups gathered around the fire, talking and laughing. "I thought she said a lot of covens had canceled."

"Yeah, well, it's cool to be a Wiccan right now. I guess everybody's doing it," Piper said, folding her arms over her chest.

"Come on, Piper, lighten up," Phoebe said, nudging her when she saw Paige's flushed reaction to Piper's comment.

"Sorry," Piper said, forcing a smile. "What do you say we split up? That way we can cover more ground."

"Sounds good," Phoebe said, clapping her hands together. "I'm goin' this way." She pointed to the right. At that moment she was actually happy to get away from her sisters before she got caught in the middle of more bickering. "Good luck, you guys!"

Phoebe started to make her way through the crowd, weaving around the covens and looking for a group to join. She couldn't believe how the covens were sticking to their own. This was supposed to be a meet-and-greet! And wasn't the whole point of this Gathering to commune with one another, learn from one another, gain strength from one another? At least, that's what it had said in the brochure Paige had printed off the Web after signing up.

"These people really need to learn how to socialize," Phoebe said under her breath.

The telltale whistle of a meathead guy cut through the din of conversation, and Phoebe stopped, realizing it was directed at her. Someone was apparently checking her out. She clenched her teeth and silently told herself not to snap. At least now she had an icebreaker. She took a deep breath, turned slowly, and found herself facing a large group of mostly good-looking guys, all of whom were dressed more like they belonged in a trendy New York City bar than at a Coven Gathering. Pressed button-down shirts, gray slacks, and well-shined shoes abounded.

One tall, broad, blond Greek-god type stepped away from the others and looked her up and down appreciatively. Phoebe rolled her eyes.

"Did you really just whistle at me?" she asked.

"You and only you, babe," the guy replied.

Repulsive, Phoebe thought. But she didn't say it. "Does that ever work?" she asked.

"Well, you stopped," the guy said with a cocky smile.

"Yes, but only because I was curious to find out exactly how few brain cells you actually had," she replied, filling her voice with false sweetness and batting her eyelashes at him.

All of the guy's friends winced and laughed and whooped. One of them slapped him on the back in glee. His face fell, but only momentarily.

"What's your name?" he asked.

"Phoebe," she replied, taking a few steps closer to the group. "And you are . . . ?"

"Craig," he replied. "I'm the high priest of this coven."

"Ah, that explains it," Phoebe said knowingly.

"Explains what?" he asked.

"Your ego complex," she replied with a smirk.

"Touché," Craig said, tilting his head slightly. "Come on, Phoebe, hang out with us."

Phoebe looked around at the guys, most of whom were watching her appreciatively, and almost walked away. After all, talking to these people could clearly turn out to be the single most annoying experience of her life. But she was supposed to be getting info here, so instead of bailing, she decided just to jump right in and get it over with before they all started coming on to her in turn.

"So, have you guys heard about the kidnappings?" she asked. "Pretty freaky, huh?"

"Yeah, we're not worried," a stocky African-American guy said, pushing up the sleeves of his turtleneck. "Let him try to take us on."

"Yeah, in case you haven't noticed, there are a lot of us," another guy with long brown hair put in. His blue eyes practically pierced through Phoebe as he spoke. "And we're pretty damn powerful. We've dedicated our lives to the Horned God. He will keep us strong."

"Well . . . that's good," Phoebe replied, having no idea what else to say. It wasn't like she could tell them that if this thing was actually a warlock or a demon, then paying homage to the Horned God, whoever he was, wasn't going to do them much good.

"Forget the kidnapper," Craig said, stepping way too close to her. She could feel his hot breath on her face, and it smelled like alcohol. "Let's talk about what's really important. Like where you and I can go to be alone."

Phoebe briefly imagined the look on this creep's face if she were to grab him and vault him clear over the fire, but she fought the urge. Instead she held up her left hand and wiggled her ring finger, and her engagement ring, in his face.

"Sorry, Craig," she said. "I'm taken."

"So?" he shot back, somehow moving even closer. "Everyone knows that anything goes at these Gatherings."

"Okay, that's my cue," Phoebe said, taking a step back. "Hopefully I won't see you guys later."

She turned on her heel and hustled away, suddenly feeling the need for a nice, long shower. That little encounter had been totally pointless and had given her a major case of the creeps. She really hoped that every guy at this

Gathering wasn't as oversexed as that one, because if that was the case, the women weren't going to stand a chance.

"Phoebe! Phoebe! Wait up!"

Some guy was jogging up behind her, but Phoebe didn't stop moving. She had a feeling it was Craig, and she couldn't be responsible for her actions if he made another move on her. She clasped her right hand over her engagement ring, wishing Cole were here right now, and silently warned Craig just to back off.

"Phoebe!"

The guy caught up to her and slid around in front of her, causing Phoebe to stop short. But when she looked up, it wasn't Craig blocking her way, but a nice-looking guy with short, dark hair and kind blue eyes. She could tell from his trendy clothes that he was part of the evil-guy coven, but she had a gut feeling he and Craig weren't exactly soul mates.

"Listen, I'm really sorry about those guys," he said, slightly out of breath. "I just wanted to let you know that we're not all like that."

"It's okay," Phoebe said, pulling her hands inside the sleeves of her sweater. "But just so you know, I wasn't walking away because I was intimidated. I was walking away to keep from leveling that Craig guy."

"I understand," he said with a laugh. "I have to do the same myself sometimes. I almost wish you *had* flattened him." He held out his hand to her and smiled. "I'm Christian. Craig and I sort of share the high priest duties. A good-Wiccan–bad-Wiccan thing, if you will."

Phoebe grinned and shook his hand. "It's nice to meet you, Christian. Thanks for coming over."

"Anytime," he said. He started to move past her to return to his coven. "Well, I guess I'll see ya."

Phoebe turned around as Christian walked away, her conscience taking over. If Christian and Craig were the high priests of their coven, they were most likely targets for the kidnapper. Especially if the coven was as powerful as the guy with the piercing eyes had bragged.

"Christian!" she called out before he got too far. He turned and looked back at her, a question in his eyes. Phoebe walked up to him and cleared her throat, stalling while she tried to find the right words. "Listen . . . you should watch your back," she said finally, keeping her voice low as members of other covens walked by in all directions. "It seems like this kidnapper is taking the most powerful member of each coven, so you and Craig are probably up there on his list."

Christian's face clouded, and he crossed his arms over his chest. "Really? The most powerful member?" he asked. "That's interesting."

"Yeah, well, I just wanted to let you know," Phoebe said with a quick smile. She turned to walk away before Christian could form any questions. Like how she had figured out the power connection. She didn't exactly want to explain her involvement with the police and have that rumor running around. She, Paige, and Piper had to try to keep a low profile.

"Thanks for the heads-up, Phoebe!" Christian called after her.

Phoebe raised her hand without looking back, then lost herself in the crowd.

"You're pretty cool, Paige," Jasmine Black said, passing Paige a little flask of alcohol she and the other girls in her coven were swigging from. "I'm glad you came over here."

"Uh . . . me, too," Paige said, handing the flask to the purple-haired girl next to her without touching it to her lips. She wasn't about to consume anything that could make her lose even the slightest bit of control. Not when there was a crazed kidnapper out there.

"Not like all the other losers at this place," the purple-haired girl said before taking a nice long drink. The rest of the coven laughed, some of them approaching actual cackles, and Paige couldn't help smiling. If nothing else, Jasmine and her friends were definitely entertaining.

When Paige had started making her way around the fire, she had felt a bit out of place. She'd passed a group of women who were holding some kind of séance, and another crowd of Renaissance Faire rejects dancing around a guy who was playing a lute. It was like all of Piper's worst nightmares had come true, and Paige was starting to wonder if her sister had been right all along. Maybe there was nothing she could learn from these people. Then she'd heard the loud laughter coming from the group of Goth girls and felt like she was coming home. They reminded her of her friends from high school—disgruntled, dysfunctional, and rowdy.

"So, where's your coven?" Jasmine asked, shaking her black curls back from her face. She had a nose ring with a purple stone and very pale skin. Paige wasn't sure if it was her actual complexion or if she'd covered herself with white powder to get the near-dead effect. It was hard to focus on *anything* in the eerie light and odd shadows cast by the bonfire.

"Oh, we decided to split up and meet people," Paige said casually.

"Well, you came to the right place. I don't know why you'd want to meet any of these other poseurs," Jasmine said snidely. "This place is just crawling with rejects. This Gathering is nothing like what I expected. No one here has any *real* power."

Paige pressed her lips together, wondering what Jasmine would think if she orbed herself out of here right now or if Piper blew something up or if Phoebe pulled her ninja act. She could show these girls some *real* power. Of course, who knew what Jasmine and her friends could do?

"Are you guys . . . I mean, do you have . . ."

"Powers?" Jasmine asked, raising her skinny black eyebrows. "Oh, yeah. We're almost afraid to show these people what we're capable of."

"Don't want to freak out the wanna-bes," Purple Hair said, elbowing Paige hard in the back and letting out another obnoxious laugh. A few of her friends joined in loudly.

"Seriously," said the girl to Jasmine's left, whose name was Sarah and who had the longest brown hair Paige had ever seen. "I bet most of the people here don't even know how to cast a magic circle."

"Or what color candles to use in a purification ceremony," Jasmine put in.

"Or where to get good bog bean," Purple Hair added with a snort. "They probably don't even know what bog bean *is*."

The other girls laughed conspiratorially, and it was all Paige could do to keep from laughing at them. She couldn't believe how elitist they were. Man, how she wanted to orb something. . . .

There was a loud shout from a crowd behind them, and both Paige and Jasmine turned to look. It was the hippie types, and they were all laughing and hooting over something a guy with a long beard had just said. A woman sat on the ground playing the guitar for a few dazed-looking spectators on the outskirts of the group, and the bearded guy suddenly started dancing like a maniac.

"Ugh! I mean, look at them!" Jasmine said, grimacing. She flicked a curl of ash from the bonfire off her sleeve with a perfectly shaped dark purple fingernail. "They're so cliché!"

Paige glanced at Jasmine out of the corner of her eye to see if she was serious, but it seemed she was. It was kind of unbelievable that the girl felt she could pick on anyone, considering that Jasmine and her friends were a bit cliché themselves. Black clothing, piercings, and pentagram tattoos abounded in the large circle. They looked like they'd just stepped out of a clearance sale at Witches "R" Us.

"So, did you guys hear about this kidnapper?" Paige asked, glancing around the circle.

"Yeah, what a psycho, huh?" Jasmine said, gazing across the circle at the bonfire.

"A smart psycho," Paige said, hugging herself. "He's grabbed, like, sixteen people and hasn't been caught."

"You sound concerned," Jasmine said, her brow creasing as she looked at Paige.

"Aren't you?" Paige asked, incredulous.

"Eh, not really," Jasmine replied with a quick shrug. "If anything, you should be worried about those hippie nuts back there. Like I said, *we* have actual powers. We can take care of our-selves."

That's what I'm worried about, Paige thought. If these girls really did have actual powers, then the kidnapper was most likely going to come after them, not after the hippie-nut wanna-bes.

"Listen, I'm gonna go find my sis—I mean, my coven," Paige said to Jasmine. "Just . . . be on the lookout for anything weird, okay?"

"Thanks for the tip," Jasmine said with a hint of sarcasm. "Don't worry about it. It's probably just some fetishist wacko. The cops will figure it out."

"Yeah . . . later," Paige said as she walked away, stepping over the prone body of one of the hippies who was either completely drunk or just a really deep sleeper. She hoped Jasmine was right. How great would it be to be dealing with a simple, human, serial kidnapper?

Unfortunately she had a feeling that was far from the truth.

"You have the most beautiful aura!"

Piper stopped in her tracks when she saw a large woman with long gray hair rushing up to her, her blue eyes open in ecstasy as she gazed at the air around Piper's head. A wreath of flow-ers sat atop her hair, and she wore a robe of pink-and-white gauze. She ran at Piper so quickly that for a moment Piper thought she was going to have to freeze the woman to keep her from tackling her to the ground. But instead she stopped just inches from Piper's face and stared all around her in a way that made Piper feel as if she weren't actually there.

"It's so full of peaceful colors!" the woman said, reaching out with her fingertips as if to gingerly touch the air next to Piper's cheek.

"That's great," Piper said, moving to get past the woman. "Thanks a lot for your time."

What a freak, she thought.

"Oh, but there's anger, too," the woman said, her voice instantly serious. She reached out and grabbed Piper's arms before Piper could step around her. "You have some black swirls here and there! That means anger."

"Uh-huh," Piper said. Like it was really difficult to tell that she was angry at the moment. She wondered if the woman could tell that the anger was directed at *her*.

"You should really do something to cleanse that," the woman said. "We have some herbs back at our tent if you'd like to—"

"No, thanks, really," Piper said. "I believe a certain level of black swirls is actually quite healthy."

The woman's eyebrows knit in confusion, and her pause gave Piper enough time to make a speedy getaway. She cut through the crowd until she was on the outskirts, where there was a bit more breathing room. So far she'd been weaving her way around the little coven groups for half an hour and hadn't gotten anywhere. She was starting to think that there was no one sane at this entire Gathering, let alone anyone approachable.

Piper walked around the outer rim of the crowd, trying to find someone, anyone, that she felt comfortable speaking with. A few people came twirling past her in a kind of spiritual conga line, and Piper stepped out of the way. Maybe it was time to call it quits and head back for the tent. On top of everything else she had a feeling she was starting to get a simulated sunburn from the fire.

She turned and made her way back toward the path that led to tent 32, already daydreaming of moisturizer and a nice long sleep. But just as she was about to make her escape she noticed two girls, each with short blond hair, huddled together in intense conversation. They were both wearing jeans and boots and regular cotton sweaters. Piper felt a strong wave of relief wash over her. Maybe she wasn't alone in this. Maybe there *were* some other normal people around here!

Piper took a step toward the girls but paused awkwardly when she heard one of them sniffling. She didn't want to butt in on a private conversation, especially if one of the girls was upset. Maybe tomorrow would be a better time. She glanced in their direction as she walked by, heading for the tent once again, and the taller girl looked up and caught Piper's eye. Piper shot her a quick smile, and the girl smiled back. That was all Piper needed for an opening.

"Hi," Piper said, raising her hand. "Everything okay?"

"Yeah," the taller girl replied, holding her elbows and casting a look at the other girl, who looked down at the ground.

"That doesn't sound too convincing," Piper said, taking a step toward them. "I'm Piper Halliwell," she said, offering her hand.

The taller girl took it and smiled. She had slightly straighter, slightly longer hair than the other girl, but they both had very clear blue eyes.

"I'm Tessa Conners," she said, shaking her straight bangs away from her face. "This is my sister Taryn," she added.

Taryn turned and shook hands with Piper as well. Piper couldn't help noticing that Taryn was cold and that her grip was fairly weak. Her choppy blond hair looked as if it hadn't been washed or combed in a while. When Piper looked into the girl's eyes, her heart turned. They were full of sorrow.

"Is everything all right?" Piper asked again, a shiver of foreboding racing over her skin.

"Well, I guess we may as well tell you," Tessa

said, looking to her sister for approval. Taryn gave a small nod and lifted one shoulder. "You've heard about the kidnappings?" Tessa continued. "Well, our little sister, Tina, was one of the victims."

"Oh, my God," Piper said, covering her heart with her hand. "I'm so sorry."

"It's okay," Taryn said quietly. "Well, I mean, it's not *okay*, but . . ."

Tessa wrapped her arm around her sister's shoulders and gave her a squeeze. "It's just one of those situations where you don't know what to say, you know?"

"I understand," Piper said. She looked around and spotted a small wooden bench outside one of the tents. "Here. Why don't we sit?" she suggested.

Taryn and Tessa followed her over to the bench, and Taryn lowered herself carefully onto the seat. She was clearly taking her sister's disappearance very hard. She was thin and frail, and Piper found herself wondering when the girl had last eaten. Not that she blamed her. She was sure that if Phoebe or Paige disappeared without a trace, she'd have some trouble eating herself.

"So . . . how long has she been missing?" Piper asked. "If you don't mind talking about it."

"Almost three weeks," Tessa replied, holding Taryn's hand. "We only came to this Gathering because Tina really wanted to come." She looked around at the frolicking people and the roaring fire and sighed. "I guess we just didn't realize how hard it would be to be here."

"Was she taken in the middle of the night like the others?" Piper asked.

"Without a trace," Taryn replied, staring at the bonfire. "The police couldn't do anything. The kidnappers didn't leave any evidence."

"So I've heard," Piper said, shifting in her seat. She had been through the drill and knew what these girls must be feeling—knowing that their sister was out there somewhere, helpless. Or worse—that she could already be dead.

"She would have loved this," Taryn said, glancing at Tessa.

"Tina was the one who got us into the Craft," Tessa explained, leaning forward to better see Piper. The light from the fire illuminated one side of her face and gave her a kind of ethereal glow. "She was more dedicated than we were. She always wanted us to be more devoted. . . ."

"She would have wanted us to be here," Taryn added. "And besides, we were going crazy at home just waiting for news."

Piper nodded, her heart breaking for the sisters. Once again it seemed that the kidnapper had chosen the most powerful of a coven, but this time he had also broken up a family.

Piper looked across the clearing, where she

quickly spotted Paige talking to one of the girls in the white gowns. At that moment she resolved to stop teasing Paige so much about wanting to be here. Paige was her sister and she loved her. The last thing she wanted was for Paige to think otherwise. And she also resolved to do everything she could to help Taryn and Tessa find out what had happened to their youngest sister.

"We'll find her," Piper said quietly. "If it's the last thing we do."

Chapter
6

Piper trudged along the path toward the dining hall the following morning in desperate need of a cup of coffee. When she'd woken half an hour earlier, Phoebe's and Paige's cots had been perfectly made and the two were nowhere in sight. She had no idea why they hadn't woken her up, but now she was late, she was cranky, and she was feeling seriously caffeine deprived. Unfortunately, even at this early hour, it seemed to be about a hundred degrees outside and her hair was already sticking to her neck, and she had a feeling that iced coffee was not going to be an option at good old Tumbleweed Campground.

Piper swung open the heavy door to the dining hall and was hit with a blessed blast of air-conditioned air. The large room was lined with long, family-style tables, and each one was packed with people. The noise level was not unlike that at a rock concert. Piper took a deep breath and looked down at her itinerary, which was marked with a table number for all meals.

"What table're ya at, little lady?"

Piper jumped at the sound of a loud, rumbling voice right at her elbow. A tall, dark-haired man with the straightest, whitest teeth she'd ever seen was smiling down at her. He wore a plaid shirt, jeans, and cowboy boots and was craning his neck to try to read over her shoulder.

"Uh, who are you?" Piper asked. Her social skills were not the best first thing in the morning.

"Sorry. Where are my manners?" he replied. "I'm Ryan Treetop, owner of this establishment." He reached out a large hand to shake with her, and Piper briefly grasped it.

"Nice to meet you. I'm Piper Halliwell," Piper said, leaning slightly away from him. His energy was a bit too much to take before she'd had her coffee. "I'm at table three."

"All righty," he said. "That'll be toward the front of the room on the left. Hope you enjoy your breakfast."

"Thanks," Piper said, moving quickly away.

She made her way down the center aisle between the tables. But when she arrived at table 3, she was looking at four Trekkie-type guys, all of whom were wearing shiny blue tops and dark black sunglasses.

"Greetings, fair Wiccan," one of the guys said, his face blank and his voice monotone. Piper wasn't even sure if he had moved his thin lips.

"Hi," Piper said warily. "Have you seen two brunette girls who look kinda like me?"

"They are at the condiment table," another one of the guys answered, just as flatly. "They seated themselves earlier at the other end of the table."

"Thanks," Piper said.

She slid by them quickly, looking over the platters and bowls on the table as she went. There was a huge fruit salad, a basket filled with all kinds of breads, a few bowls of jam and butter, and a large platter of scrambled eggs. But no coffee. Where was the coffee?

Piper plopped down at an empty plate at the far end of the table. Across from her were two more plates filled with fruit and muffins, and between them was a large book titled *The Wiccan Handbook*. Piper did her best to keep from groaning. The last thing she wanted was to break her be-nice-to-Paige resolution before she even had a chance to keep it. But she needed her coffee now, or her cranky side was going to take over.

Finally she saw Phoebe and Paige approaching from the other side of the room, and she almost shouted out in joy. Paige was carrying three steaming mugs. What would she do without her sisters?

"Good morning, sunshine!" Paige said, placing one of the mugs down in front of Piper. "Thought you could use a pick-me-up."

"Thank you, thank you, thank you," Piper said, inhaling the comforting caffeinated scent. She leaned into the table and reached for the sugar bowl, then dropped back into her seat. "By the way, why didn't you *wake* me up?" she asked, spooning out a heap of sugar.

Phoebe and Paige exchanged a look as they sat down across from Piper. "Uh . . . we tried," Paige said. "You don't remember?"

"What are you talking about?" Piper asked as she stirred her coffee. "No, you didn't."

"Piper, you threatened to blow us up, so we thought it best to leave you alone," Phoebe said quietly.

"I did not!" Piper said with a laugh.

"Well, I guess that means you were asleep, which is probably a good thing," Paige said, smiling. "That means it was just your subconscious talking and you don't *actually* want to kill us. Of course, I don't know how Leo deals with *that* every morning."

Phoebe giggled and popped a grape into her mouth as she opened the Wicca book. Piper eyed her curiously. She'd figured the book belonged to Paige. What was going on here? Was Phoebe going over to the dark side as well?

"Phoebe, what're you doing?" Piper asked.

"Oh, I have to write that thing for the rededication ceremony, so I'm just trying to get an idea of what it's all about," Phoebe said, her nose in the book. "This is actually kind of interesting."

Piper saw Paige shoot her a wary glance, clearly waiting for her to start in on the whole Wiccans-are-fakes thing again. Instead Piper bit her tongue and busied herself with dishing up some fruit onto her plate. But she hated keeping her opinion to herself when she knew she was right. Why bother wasting time writing something for a ceremony that didn't mean anything? None of this had anything to do with the evil she and her sisters put their lives on the line to fight every single day.

"Well, the good news is nothing suspicious happened last night," Paige said as she buttered a muffin. "No one's reported anything, anyway."

That's probably because the kidnapper is smart enough to know that no one who would come to this thing has any real power, Piper thought. *He probably couldn't be bothered.* After seeing all the crazies around the campfire the night before, and hearing about the egotistical poseurs her sisters had met, she was starting to think this whole plan would turn out to be a bust.

"Piper? Are you okay?" Paige asked, her forehead wrinkling as she bit into a blueberry muffin. "You look a little tense."

Don't say it! Don't say it! Piper told herself. But she couldn't seem to stop her mouth from opening. She was about to let it all spill out, when she saw Taryn and Tessa coming toward the table and managed to stop herself. Just in the nick of time.

"Hey, Piper!" Tessa said with a smile. "You're at table three, too?"

"Hi, guys!" Piper said, relieved to have something else to distract her. "I guess this is where they put the smaller groups. Taryn and Tessa, these are my sisters, Phoebe and Paige."

Everyone said hello, and Piper and her sisters slid down to make room for Taryn and Tessa, both of whom looked a bit better this morning. Taryn was still a little pale, but she had her short hair pushed back in a headband, and she appeared more rested than she had last night. Piper was also happy to see that she at least had her appetite back. She dished up a ton of fruit for herself, and Tessa went off to get them both some tea. Phoebe put the Wicca book aside, and Piper started to relax.

"So, Taryn, we were very sorry to hear about what happened to your sister," Phoebe said, folding her hands on the table. "Piper filled us in last night."

"Thank you," Taryn said with a small smile. "We really miss her."

"Did you hear anything the night she disappeared?" Paige asked. "Anything at all?"

"No," Taryn answered, her eyes darting toward her sister, who was returning to the table. "Actually, if you don't mind, I'd rather not talk about it."

Piper felt as if a rock were hardening in the pit of her stomach, and Paige shot her a guilty glance.

"Of course, sweetie. We understand," Piper said, reaching across the table to touch Taryn's hand. She looked up at Piper and smiled for real for the first time since they met. Piper's heart went out to her all over again.

"Everything okay?" Tessa asked, hovering at the end of the table.

Before anyone could answer, the double doors at the entrance of the dining hall were flung open so hard they slammed back against the walls, causing a terrifying clatter. A short but muscular African-American guy came barreling into the room, his eyes wild.

"Craig's missing!" he exclaimed, looking over at a table filled with guys who seemed to Piper more like a bunch of stockbrokers than Wiccans. They had to be members of the coven Phoebe had told her about last night. The table fell silent, and Piper could feel the tension and fear fill the room. The guy looked around, his eyes traveling over Tessa, who was the only person standing, and falling on Phoebe, when they inexplicably hardened.

"Where is he?" the guy asked.

"I have no idea," Phoebe said, getting to her feet. "But we'll find him."

"All right, all right, everyone stay calm," Ryan Treetop said, stepping up next to the guy who had made the announcement. "What we need here is a plan."

At that moment a tall guy with brown hair stood up from the stockbroker table and looked at Phoebe, his expression scared but confident at the same time. "Everyone fan out. If Craig is somewhere on this campground, I want him found."

The sounds of scraping chairs and fretful whispers took over as everyone in the room started to file out. Piper saw Ryan walk to the front of the room to intercept Marcia Farina before she could leave. His face was flushed and he definitely didn't look happy as he pulled her aside to speak with her. Piper had a feeling he was a bit worried about what the news of a kidnapping on the property might do to his business.

"Oh, God," Taryn said, looking up at her sister with tears in her eyes. "It's happening again!"

"You two stay here," Piper said, resting her hand on Tessa's back as she stood. "We have enough people looking, and you don't have to put yourselves through this."

She grabbed Phoebe and Paige and hustled out of the dining hall through one of the back doors, where there were fewer people. The moment they were outside, they huddled near the wall.

"What was that all about?" Piper asked Phoebe. "Why did that guy look at you like that?"

"This Craig person is the one who came on to me last night in front of all his friends," Phoebe replied, rubbing her forehead. "I don't know, I guess he was just thinking about that. But you guys, Craig is the high priest of that coven," she added, her eyes wide with fear. "If the kidnapper knew that—"

"Then he was a prime target," Paige said. "Come on. Let's go to his tent and see what we can find."

Paige led the way toward the tents, but the mayhem on the grounds didn't make for an easy trek. Members of Craig's coven were barking out orders to other Wiccans and every tent was being searched. The desperation and fear in the air was starting to make people panic. Piper couldn't help thinking of the witch hunts she'd read so much about since finding out a few years ago she and her sisters were witches. But this time witches were violating witches.

"This is not good," Piper said when she saw one of Craig's brethren tossing clothes and bedding out of one of the tents. "We have to stop this."

"There!" Phoebe said, pointing at a tent that had two guys standing outside of it, apparently acting as guards. "That has to be it."

The three sisters walked up to the sentries, and Phoebe took a step forward. "Hey, we'd like to get a look inside," she said to the taller of the two guys. He had long hair and seriously mean-looking blue eyes.

"I don't think so," he said firmly. "Christian said no one is to go in until we find Craig."

"Okay, fine," Paige said, pulling on Phoebe's arm. "Let's go . . . *find Craig*." She tilted her head to tell Piper and Phoebe to follow her, then led them around to the back of the tent. "All right," she said, holding both their hands. "We're going in."

Before Piper could even utter a protest, she was enveloped in Paige's white light and reappeared with her sisters inside the tent.

"Paige!" Piper exclaimed. "If anyone saw you—"

"Don't worry. There was no one back there," Paige said, glancing around. "Hey! Why does he get his own tent?" she whispered indignantly. Sure enough, there was only one cot in this tent, but it was practically destroyed. One leg was crushed, the sheets and blankets were shredded and tossed around the room, and the pillow looked like someone had used a machete on it.

"He was on the prowl last night," Phoebe reminded them. "Maybe he paid extra so he could have some privacy and lure the ladies back to his lair."

"What is this?" Piper asked, taking a few steps closer to the bed. Slashes of some shiny black substance covered the mattress, and there were even a few on the canvas wall next to the cot. Piper touched one of the marks with the tip of her finger and rubbed it against her thumb. "It has the consistency of oil," she said, scrunching up her nose. She sniffed her fingers, and the sour, tangy smell made her stomach heave.

"Ugh! But it doesn't *smell* like oil," she added. "I have no idea what that is." She wiped her hands on the sheets and stepped away from the bed.

"Whatever did this must have had some serious claws," Phoebe said. "This is weird, right? I mean, there wasn't any evidence at the other kidnappings, and now we have this."

"And I don't remember a mention of shredded bedding, either," Paige said, holding a strip of torn sheet between two fingers.

Suddenly there were loud male voices outside the tent, and Phoebe grabbed her sisters' arms.

"That's Christian," she said. "We better get out of here."

Paige orbed them out of the tent and back into their own so that no one would see them. The second they were there, Piper grabbed her cell phone and started dialing.

"Who are you calling?" Paige asked.

"Daryl," Piper said, clutching the phone. She'd promised to keep him updated if even the slightest thing was amiss, and this new evidence was a lot more than slight.

"Detective Morris," Daryl's voice barked on the other end of the line.

"Daryl, it's Piper. We've had a kidnapping," Piper said, lowering herself onto her cot shakily. "Was there anything about oily black markings with the other victims?"

"No. Nothing like that," Daryl said. "Are you telling me this guy finally left evidence? Maybe he's getting careless."

"I'm definitely thinking it's more of an *it* than a *he*," Piper told him, looking up at her sisters. "I'm gonna call Leo."

"All right," Daryl said. "Just let me know if you find anything else, and please be careful."

"We will," Piper said. She clicked off the phone. "Leo!" she shouted at the top of her lungs, expending some of her pent-up tension and causing Paige and Phoebe to jump.

Leo instantly orbed into the tent and looked

around at the sisters. "That was a loud one," he said. "What's going on?"

"Another kidnapping," Paige replied, hugging her arms to herself. "Not pretty."

Piper stood and dropped her phone on the bed. She was so tense she couldn't even let herself be comforted at the sight of her husband. "Can you check the Book of Shadows for anything that might kidnap witches and leave behind oily black markings?" she asked him.

"Sure," Leo replied, his brow creased. "But it could be a little while. The Elders are keeping us pretty busy. You know, with all the kidnappings . . ."

"Just do what you can, okay?" Piper asked.

"I will," Leo said. He gave her a quick hug and kissed her forehead and was gone.

"It's gonna be okay," Phoebe said, coming over and wrapping her arms around Piper. "Thanks to those black marks, we're a lot closer to finding this thing."

Paige joined in on the group hug, and Piper closed her eyes, trying to blot out the images of all those ripped sheets, all those marks. Trying to blot out the thought of Taryn and Tessa's little sister in the hands of whatever this thing was.

Trying to blot out the thought that one of the Charmed Ones could be next.

● ● ●

That night Phoebe stood outside the tent, watching the mass exodus that seemed to be taking place. Craig hadn't been found, and each passing moment that he was still missing seemed to drive the population of the Gathering a little more crazy with worry. The hippie coven that was staying in the next few tents was on its way out. They had backed up their two vans right near their tent doors and were randomly throwing things inside.

Marcia stood outside a tent a few plots down, arguing with one of the Trekkie guys from Phoebe's table in the dining hall.

"Look, I think we deserve a full refund here," the guy said, no longer using the affected one-note voice he'd had that morning. "You don't even know what happened to this guy! And you don't even have security!"

"I'm cooperating with the police, and they're going to station a few officers here," Marcia said desperately. "Please, I'm sure there will be no more incidents."

"There's already been one too many," the guy said firmly. "We're leaving, and if I don't get my money back when I stop by Treetop's office in ten minutes, then you'll both be hearing from my lawyer."

Phoebe sighed as the guy stalked back into his tent and Marcia scurried off, frazzled and upset. This wasn't exactly turning out to be the peaceful Gathering everyone expected. Craig's kidnapping wasn't Marcia's fault, but Phoebe couldn't help agreeing with the Trekkie guy. One incident was one too many.

A few other covens had already pulled out early that afternoon. Those who were sticking it out were busy using incense and crystals to cast protection circles around their tents. The atmosphere was more subdued than it had been that morning, but it was also grim. As if everyone had resolved themselves to the fact that it was going to happen again.

Phoebe took a deep breath and walked back inside the tent. Paige was lying on her cot reading her handbook, and Piper was refolding her clothes.

"What is that *smell*?" Piper asked, looking up at Phoebe.

"Incense," Phoebe replied, crossing to her cot and pulling her bag out from underneath. She unzipped the outside pocket and pulled out five crystals she'd packed at the last minute. They clinked together in her palm, and their cool, smooth surface made her feel a bit better.

"What are you doing?" Piper asked as Paige sat up on her own cot.

"I think we should cast a protection circle," Phoebe said, walking out the tent door. She placed one crystal right in front of it on the ground, then walked around the tent, placing the other crystals in a circle. Piper and Paige came out and watched her as she worked.

"Do you really think this is necessary?" Piper asked, folding her arms over her chest.

"Of course it is," Phoebe said, her breath starting to come fast and shallow. "Piper, you were as freaked as everyone else this morning, if not more so."

"I know that," Piper said. "But Phoebe, we have protections these other people don't have. If something with huge claws busts into our tent, I'll just blow it up." She said the last few words quietly so that the packing hippies wouldn't hear. "Besides, these things have flaws. If there were one foolproof protection spell, we'd have one on the manor and we wouldn't be getting threatened every five minutes."

"It's better than nothing," Phoebe said firmly.

"Well, I for one am with Phoebe," Paige said, reaching out and taking Phoebe's hand. "I'd rather the claw thing never make it into the tent at all."

"Fine," Piper said, rolling her eyes and holding hands with Paige. "Let's do this quickly before anyone notices." Together the three of them recited the words to a simple protection spell:

> "Through this circle the Charmed Ones cast,
> Let no one beyond our trust pass."

• • •

A flash of purple light illuminated the circle defined by the crystals, then disappeared. Phoebe looked around to see if anyone had noticed, but the other covens were too busy with their own spells. No one even glanced in their direction.

"Thanks, guys," Phoebe said, letting out a little sigh of relief. "I feel much better."

"Good," Piper said, rubbing Phoebe's back. "I guess it's best to do everything we can."

"Okay, I say it's time to hit the Strip," Paige said, dropping Phoebe's hand. She ducked back through the door flap, and Phoebe and Piper followed. Paige grabbed her lipstick and a mirror and quickly applied a new coat, then smacked her lips together. "I saw Taryn and Tessa earlier, and they said they wanted to get away from all the mayhem, so . . . what do you say?"

"Sounds good to me," Phoebe said with a grin. "I could use a vacation from this vacation." She and Paige both looked at Piper. "Are you in?"

"I am so in," Piper said, grabbing her own bag. "Let's get the heck out of here!"

Paige stalked through the casino, an empty plastic bucket in her hand, waving aside clouds of cigarette and cigar smoke. The place was like a labyrinth of blinking lights, whirling slots, and waitresses in absurdly little clothing. Every time she took a turn, she was sure she was going down the aisle of slot machines where she'd last seen her sisters, and every time she was greeted by the sight of another ten to twenty tired, annoyed strangers. If everyone was having so little fun, then why did it seem like their butts were permanently attached to the little velvet chairs?

"Okay, I give up," Paige said aloud, throwing up her arms.

"You give up what?" Phoebe's voice asked.

Paige turned to see her sisters standing on their tiptoes to peer over the next row of slots. Heaving a sigh of relief, Paige walked over to them and slapped her empty cup down between two machines.

"I don't understand what everyone thinks is so great about this place," she said, crossing her arms over her chest and sitting on the empty chair next to Phoebe. "This stopped being fun about five minutes ago."

"What happened five minutes ago?" Piper asked, raising one eyebrow. She had to lean forward to see Paige past Phoebe.

"I lost my last twenty dollars," Paige replied grumpily. She felt like such a moron. She knew she should have stopped herself before putting that last twenty in the machine, but it was like she was possessed. She couldn't stop herself from trying just one more time. . . . And now it was all gone!

"Well, I'm having a great time," Phoebe said with a laugh, holding forth her own winnings cup, which was almost full of quarters. Paige's eyes widened. There had to be at least a hundred dollars in there.

"Where did you get all that?" Paige asked.

"This is my lucky machine!" Phoebe said brightly. She patted the side of the slot machine in front of her lovingly, like it was her pet dog.

Paige leaned over and grabbed a quarter out of Phoebe's bucket, then slid it into the slot machine in front of her. She pulled the lever, closed her eyes, and said a little prayer. She just wanted to win *something* tonight. Even if it was just fifty cents. When she opened her eyes again, the slots were just stopping—cherry, cherry . . .

Paige looked at her sisters, holding her breath. One more cherry and she'd be rich! Or she'd at least break even. The last slot stopped rolling, and the line was right between a cherry and a bar. Paige's heart dropped.

"Great," she said, slumping back in her chair. "Can't we just use a little spell on this thing so I can make my money back?"

All she got in reply was two stern looks.

"Fine," Paige said, rolling her eyes.

At that moment a loud cheer sounded from at least a dozen voices somewhere in the casino. Paige could hear the sounds of high-fiving and giggles. Suddenly she felt intensely jealous that someone in this place was winning. She shook her head, unable to believe the effect the casino had on her. She was becoming a money-grubbing psycho, and they'd been here for only an hour.

"What happened to Tessa and Taryn?" Paige asked as Phoebe pulled the lever on her machine again.

"They were tired, so they went back to camp," Piper said. "Actually, I might do that myself soon."

"Sounds like a plan," Paige said. "I'm beyond bored."

Phoebe let out a squeal, and a bell started ringing loudly. The light on top of her machine blinked like crazy, and out of nowhere money started dropping into the metal tray. Paige couldn't believe it. Her sister had just gotten three cherries!

"Oh, my God! Phoebe!" Paige said, grinning.

"A thousand quarters!" Phoebe shouted, clapping. "How much is that?"

"That's two hundred fifty dollars!" Piper exclaimed as she stood and squeezed Phoebe's shoulders. "You keep going and you're going to pay for this whole vacation."

Another loud cheer went up from the middle of the casino, and Paige glanced over her sisters' heads to see if she could spot where the action was. Phoebe's machine was still slowly spitting out quarters, and Phoebe and Piper started digging them out into cups.

"You guys look like you're going to be here for a while," Paige said. "I'm gonna go check this out."

"Okay!" Phoebe said. "But hurry back! We may need help carrying all of this!"

Paige smiled and wandered off toward the cheers. She came out into the center of the casino, where all the blackjack and craps tables were. Another cheer sounded out, and Paige spotted Jasmine and all her friends hugging and jumping up and down by one of the roulette tables. They looked completely out of place in their all-black gear, and a couple of little old men in pastel shirts eyed them warily as they passed them by. Paige arrived just as the croupier was paying out a heap of chips to Purple Hair Girl.

"What's going on?" Paige asked, slipping in next to Jasmine.

"We are roulette goddesses, that's what's going on," Jasmine said, her eyes bright. It was clear in the casino light that her complexion was, in fact, whiter than white. "Check it out." She held up her own pile of chips, and Paige quickly did the math. Jasmine had more than a thousand dollars sitting in front of her.

"Damn, girl. Have you guys got a system or

something?" Paige asked as the other girls placed their bets for the next spin.

Jasmine leaned in close to Paige's ear. "Yeah. It's called magic," she said.

Paige's stomach did a little flip as Jasmine pulled away, her dark eyes sparking with mischief. Was she serious? Were they really using a spell or something to control the wheel? *Apparently these girls have never heard of the perils of personal gain,* Paige thought.

The croupier waved his hand over the roulette board, indicating that he would take no more bets, then he reached up to spin the wheel. The moment he did, Jasmine and her friends joined hands and closed their eyes. Paige could tell they were all muttering something in unison, but their lips were barely moving. The croupier was pale and a little sweaty and nervous. He looked over his shoulder as if planning a mode of escape.

The wheel stopped and the ball bounced around, finally coming to rest on black fifteen. Jasmine and her friends dropped their hands, opened their eyes, and cheered.

"Black fifteen. We have a winner," the croupier said with not an ounce of enthusiasm. He paid off a girl at the end of the table who had her own considerable pile of chips.

"What are you guys doing?" Paige whispered in Jasmine's ear.

"It's a simple manipulation spell," Jasmine replied under her breath. "With this many Wiccans doing the same incantation, it will never fail. We're just taking turns winning, that's all."

"Isn't that kind of like cheating?" Paige asked, her face growing warm.

"God, Paige," Jasmine said with a scoff. "Who knew you were such a square?"

At that moment an official-looking man with salt-and-pepper hair stepped up behind the croupier and whispered something in his ear. The croupier looked relieved, and he shot Jasmine and her friends a look that was somehow triumphant before stepping aside so the suited man could take his place at the table.

"I'm sorry, but I'm going to have to cut you girls off," the man said, his fingertips pressing into the felt top of the table. "Congratulations on your winnings, ladies, but you've cleaned out this station." He didn't crack a smile once.

"Hey! You can't tell us when to stop betting!" Purple Hair Girl shouted.

"No, no, it's all right," Jasmine said, gathering up her chips. "We were going to go to that club anyway, right, girls?"

Everyone grudgingly stacked their winnings and moved away from the table. Paige was about to say good-bye and go find her sisters again. She had to tell them what she had just witnessed. If Jasmine's coven was able to control the roulette wheel with a chant, then they obviously had *some* power. They could be next on the kidnapper's hit list. But when she turned around, Piper and Phoebe were already approaching, loaded down with full winnings cups.

"Oh, hey!" Jasmine said, tossing her curls over her shoulder. "Looks like we weren't the only big winners tonight!"

Paige laughed, stopping herself from questioning Jasmine's use of the word *winners* after she and her friends had clearly cheated.

"Piper, Phoebe, this is Jasmine," Paige said. "She and her friends just went a little crazy at the roulette wheel."

"I went a little crazy at the slots," Phoebe said proudly.

"Cool. Wanna go blow it with us? We're heading over to this new club down the Strip. It's supposed to be hot," Jasmine said. The rest of her coven was gathered at the end of the roulette table waiting for her, and Paige swore she heard one of them grumble her disapproval at the invitation Jasmine had made. Probably Purple Hair Girl.

"Well, I'm in," Paige asked. "I'm tired of the casino, but I'm too hyper to sleep."

She looked at her sisters hopefully. Paige didn't mind the idea of hanging out with Jasmine and her friends. She had a feeling they'd be a lot of fun at a dance club, since they seemed to be a bit on the wild side, but she knew she'd have a better time if Phoebe and Piper came along.

"What do you think?" Paige said, waggling her eyebrows. "We can do some sisterly bonding on the dance floor."

"I don't know," Piper said, scratching at her forehead. "I kind of want to go home and call Leo."

"Yeah, me too," Phoebe said. "Call Cole, that is."

"Come on, you guys! We're on vacation!" Paige protested. "Don't be such old married people!"

"Sorry, Paige," Piper said. "But if that's what I am, I just have to accept it."

"All right," Paige said with a little laugh. "But I'm gonna go."

Phoebe shot Piper a look. "Paige, can I see you over here for a second?" she asked, tilting her head, since she had neither hand free.

"I'll be right back," Paige told Jasmine.

"Okay, but hurry up. The natives are getting restless," Jasmine said, joining her friends.

Paige followed Piper and Phoebe over to an out-of-order change machine. Phoebe adjusted the buckets in her arms and looked at Paige. Suddenly Paige had the feeling she was in for a lecture.

"I don't think splitting up is such a good idea with this psycho on the loose," Phoebe said under her breath.

"Phoebe, come on," Paige replied. "I'll be with friends."

She swallowed back the little wave of fear that hit her at Phoebe's words. After all, she had just concluded that Jasmine could be a target for the kidnapper. But he wasn't going to take her in the middle of a raging club, so there was no reason, at the moment, to tell her sisters about her suspicions. Not when she knew they would freak out and drag her right back to the campsite.

"Yeah, she'll be fine," Piper said.

"Piper! I thought you'd be on my side with this!" Phoebe exclaimed.

"Well, for once I'm not going to be Responsible Piper," she replied, pushing her hair behind her ears. "I think Paige should go out and have fun. Besides, she's going to be surrounded by people. She'll be fine."

"Thank you!" Paige said, giving a little jump of excitement. "Tell Cole and Leo I said hi!"

Then, before Phoebe could protest any more, Paige turned and jogged over to Jasmine. It was time to have a little fun on this vacation!

Chapter
7

"**Oh, God.** What's going on?" Phoebe asked, her stomach turning as Piper drove the convertible toward the entrance to the campground. There were two cop cars parked right near the Tumbleweed Campground sign with their lights flashing. A couple of uniformed police officers stood alongside their cars, talking with their heads bent close together, the brims of their large hats touching.

"Do you think someone else is missing?" Phoebe added.

"I guess we're going to find out," Piper said as one of the police officers flashed an extremely bright flashlight at their car. He held up one hand to tell them to stop, and Piper slowed down, coming to a stop right next to him.

"Evening, ladies," the cop said, turning off the light. "State your business here, please."

"We're staying here for the . . . uh . . . convention," Piper said, shooting Phoebe a look. Phoebe knew her sister was avoiding the word *Gathering* because she was afraid of sounding like a kook.

"Well, we have some officers on site dealing with a situation," the policeman said, taking a step back. "If you'll just go directly to your tent, it would be much appreciated."

"Situation?" Phoebe said. "Is someone else missing?"

"Sorry, ma'am," he replied. "I'm not authorized to divulge any information. Just proceed to your tent."

Phoebe and Piper exchanged a disturbed glance as the officer stepped aside and waved Piper forward. She pulled the car into the dirt driveway and started carefully down the road through the dark.

"We're not actually going to our tent, right?" Piper asked, gripping the steering wheel.

"Like you even have to ask," Phoebe deadpanned.

The drive to the actual campground felt like it took forever as Phoebe tried to keep herself from thinking the worst. When they arrived, there were little clumps of people standing in front of tents and sitting on benches, talking quietly and looking over their shoulders into the dark. There was a thick, almost palpable sense of tension in the air. Piper drove right up to Treetop's office, where two more cop cars were parked, and killed the engine.

"If anyone's going to know what's going on, it's going to be Marcia," Piper said, slamming her car door and walking around the front.

"What are you going to do? Just walk right in when they're in the middle of an investigation?" Phoebe asked, scurrying to catch up.

Piper replied by doing just that. Phoebe followed, but the moment she walked into the tiny cabin office, a chubby, balding police officer grabbed her by the arms.

"You can't be in here, girls," he said, shooting Piper a semimenacing glance. "Why don't you wait outside?"

Phoebe's eyes traveled over the office quickly. Two more officers were standing near a TV and VCR in the corner, while another spoke to Marcia and Ryan Treetop behind the desk. Marcia's skin looked pale and her hair was all mussed, as if she hadn't looked in a mirror all day, and Ryan's forehead was creased with worry.

"Marcia? Is everything all right?" Phoebe asked, the cop still gripping her arms.

Marcia looked up, her eyes heavy, and it took her a moment to focus on Phoebe. "Yes, dear. The police have just confiscated a surveillance tape."

The cop released Phoebe, and her hands

instinctively flew to her biceps to rub the sore
spots where he had grabbed her. She looked
over at Piper, knowing her sister was thinking
the same thing she was. *A surveillance tape?* If
whatever had taken Craig was on that recording
and they could get a look at it, then finding the
demon in the Book of Shadows would be a lot
easier. It was always a plus to have a supernatu-
ral mug shot.

"Ms. Farina, I told you that information was
not for public knowledge," the police officer
with the serious grip said.

"I'm sorry," Marcia replied, clutching her
hands together. "It's just been a bit of a hard day."

"Can we see the tape?" Piper asked, glancing
at the VCR, which appeared to be paused on a
black-and-white shot of one of the many paths
that traversed the campground.

"No, you cannot," the police officer said con-
descendingly, his nostrils flaring slightly. "This is
official police business, and this tape is official
evidence. Now, if you two would kindly leave—"

"All righty, then," Piper said. She raised her
hands and with one swift flick of her wrists
froze the room. The police officer stopped with
his mouth half open and his eyes half closed,
and Marcia was frozen mid-weep. But most
importantly, both of the cops in the corner had
stepped far enough away from the TV for Piper
and Phoebe to access it.

"Okay, let's go," Piper said, rushing over to the VCR. She pressed Play, and she and Phoebe both stepped back to watch.

The scene flickered to life in grainy black and white. It was an angle from above on a pathway between three tents. The timer in the bottom left-hand corner read 2:43 A.M. Phoebe held her breath waiting for something to happen, but a couple of minutes passed and they saw nothing. It was just a picture of an empty path.

"I'm gonna fast-forward," she said, pressing the button. "We don't have enough time to watch the nothing hour."

The tape flew ahead with little but white tracking lines flying across the screen. Then, suddenly, Phoebe saw movement in the top left-hand corner of the screen. She jumped forward and hit the Play button.

The timer now read 2:59 A.M. Three figures, inhumanly tall and wearing long black robes, moved onto the path from the top of the screen. Phoebe felt her heart pound with foreboding. The creatures moved slowly, deliberately, and they all kept their heads down. Something about the way they moved, almost as if they were float-ing, and the way their robes swished back and forth like a whisper, sent a chill down her spine.

"What are they?" she muttered, narrowing her eyes.

"I have no idea," Piper replied. "They could

be humans. Freakishly large, NBA-prospect humans."

Then one of the creatures raised its face, and Phoebe's hand shot out to grab Piper's arm. It had a large, shiny jackal's head with a long snout and blank, staring eyes. When it bowed its head again, it reached up to pull its hood down farther over its face, and Phoebe could see as clear as day that it had large black claws.

"Okay, that's freaky," Phoebe said, releasing Piper's arm shakily as the creatures passed all the way through the shot.

"What's freaky is that those things were walking around here last night while we were sleeping," Piper said with a shudder. "Okay, quick, rewind the tape. Now at least we know what they look like."

"Are we gonna leave it here?" Phoebe asked, hitting the Rewind button.

"We have to. The guy just put it in the VCR. If we take it, they're gonna be too suspicious," Piper said, going back to stand where she'd been before she froze everyone. "Besides, they're just gonna think that somebody dressed up like that last night. No one but us is going to realize those things are real."

"Okay," Phoebe said. She stopped the tape, hit Play, and then paused it again. Then she rushed into position next to Piper. "Do it," she said.

Piper raised her hands, and at that moment the door to the office was flung open. Phoebe had just enough time to get a glimpse of Taryn, Tessa, and Christian walking in before Piper unfroze the scene.

Tessa's and Christian's eyes nearly popped out of their skulls, and Taryn had to grab on to the doorjamb for support. Phoebe wanted to throw up right then and there. Every last one of them had just witnessed Piper's power.

"—the office now," the cop said, finishing the sentence he'd started before being frozen. Then he looked past them at the three new visitors and his face reddened. "Where the hell did you three come from?" he spit.

"Come on," Piper said, grabbing Taryn's and Tessa's arms. "We were just leaving."

She pulled them out the door, and Phoebe made sure Christian walked out ahead of her so he wouldn't be able to ask any questions of the people inside the office. As soon as they were back out on the path, however, Christian was *full* of questions.

"What was that?" he demanded wildly. "What did we just see in there?"

"Nothing," Piper said automatically. "I didn't see anything weird, Phoebe, did you?"

"Nice try," Christian said, crossing his arms over his chest. "You did something to those people, and if you don't tell me what's going on right now, I'm gonna go in there and tell those cops what I just saw."

Phoebe looked at Piper, and Piper simply bowed her head, kicking at the ground with her boot and seeming very intent on watching herself do it. Phoebe opened her mouth to speak, but nothing came out. She didn't have a clue as to what she could possibly say to fix this situation.

"So, I'm going," Christian said, making a move toward the door to Treetop's cabin.

"Wait!" Tessa said, touching his arm and stopping him. She turned slowly to Piper and Phoebe and took a deep breath. "You guys, you have to tell us what's going on," she said. "Who has powers like that?"

When Piper lifted her face once more, she and Phoebe exchanged a look of grim resignation. Suddenly Phoebe found herself wishing that she and Piper had opted to hang out with Paige. At that moment she knew it was going to be a *very* long night.

Paige looked in the grungy mirror in the bathroom at the club Jasmine and her friends had brought her to, wondering why she hadn't just gone home with her sisters. Even if they were just chatting with their men, they had to be having a better time than she was. The driving beat of the dance music pounded through the walls, causing the dim light fixtures to shake and piercing Paige's temples with each downbeat. Apparently she couldn't party like she used to.

"Um, excuse me? Are you gonna hog that mirror all night?"

Paige glanced at her reflection and saw an overly made-up girl of about twenty-one standing behind her in a shimmery silver halter and boots that practically went up to her navel. Just another obnoxious girl who thought the world revolved around her and thus should get mirror time when she needed it. This whole club was packed with them. Part of Paige felt like putting this girl in her place, but a bigger part was just too tired to deal. She moved away from the sinks and shoved through the door, rejoining the throbbing crowd on the dance floor.

Almost instantly two girls came running toward the bathroom and slammed right into Paige, nearly mowing her down. Neither of them stopped to apologize, and from the way they continued to giggle and gab, Paige was fairly certain they hadn't even noticed. A group of guys in dark, trendy clothing stood near the wall and sipped beer from long-necked bottles. They eyed Paige appreciatively, and she glanced away. She had to get lost on the dance floor before one of them tried to hit on her.

Paige held her breath and dived into the mass of moving bodies, trying to make her way across the hardwood floor toward the bar, where she'd last seen Jasmine and the others. She was pretty ready to pack it in, but she wanted to tell them that she was leaving. Not that they'd notice her absence, or care, but part of her still wanted someone to know where she was and where she wasn't. Apparently her older sisters' sense of responsibility was wearing off on her.

Paige finally emerged on the other side of the dance floor, only slightly bruised, and took a deep breath. Glancing around, she saw Purple Hair Girl, whose name had turned out to be Chloe, talking to Annie of the long hair and Jesse, who was tiny, quiet, and seemed to look up to the other girls like they were her heroes. They were standing by the bar, and they were all giggling about something. Paige walked over and slipped into a tight spot between Chloe's back and a couple of people who were making out as if they were in their own bedroom and not a public place.

"Hey! Have you guys seen Jasmine?" Paige shouted at the top of her lungs to be heard over the driving dance beat.

"Paige! You are never going to believe what I just did!" Chloe said, turning around and taking a long sip of her martini. "You see that guy over by the wall? The one in the hideous black-and-gray shirt?" She pointed across the dance floor to a geeky-looking guy in a retro top and black pants who was surveying the dance floor. His hair was pulled back in a ponytail, and he wore one long earring.

"Yeah, what about him?" Paige asked, trying to ignore the hint of foreboding in her chest.

"Well, he was totally coming on to Jesse and would not leave her alone, so I marked him," Chloe said, smirking mischievously before taking another slug of her drink.

"You marked him?" Paige repeated. She had no idea what it meant to mark someone, but it didn't sound like a good thing.

"Yeah. I keep this potion in my bag in case I ever need it," Chloe said, slipping a vial out of her slim black bag. "All you've gotta do is put some on your fingertip and wipe it across the back of a person's neck. It's like instant beer goggles." She glanced over Paige's shoulder and laughed. "See! Check it out!"

The geeky guy was coming on strong to an overweight girl in an extremely tight bodysuit. He had her pinned up against the wall and was running his finger down her cheek lovingly. The girl looked totally uncomfortable and was finally able to inch herself away from the guy. Paige felt sick to her stomach. She couldn't believe Chloe had worked a spell on the poor guy. And it wasn't exactly fair to the female population of the club, either. He was probably going to come on to every girl present before the end of the night.

"That's not funny, Chloe," Paige said. She was beginning to feel like she was dealing with kindergartners. Chloe's face darkened, and Paige knew she was about to tell her off, but before she could, Jasmine returned, laughing and squealing excitedly.

"I got it! I got a piece of her hair!" Jasmine said, holding out two pinched fingers.

"Perfect!" Chloe exclaimed. She dropped the vial of potion back into her bag and pulled out a tiny white voodoo doll. "Here! Give it to me."

"You're gonna love this one, Paige," Annie said, leaning her elbows into the bar.

Chloe wrapped a piece of long, almost white blond hair around the doll's neck until it was tight. Then she held the doll in both hands and recited quickly, "With my words this doll becomes my instrument. Give me the power to work my magic on she whose hair here lies."

Chloe grinned at Paige, who started to squirm uncomfortably, then placed the doll on the bar. "Ready, girls?" Chloe asked conspiratorially.

Annie, Jesse, Chloe, and Jasmine all placed one finger on the doll and looked across the room toward the bathroom. Paige glanced around, but no one seemed to be paying any attention to what was going on. There was too much mayhem in the room to take it all in. Besides, even if someone did see Jasmine and her friends working voodoo, they probably

wouldn't think much of it. This town was filled
with more bizarre people than San Francisco.

"Who is this spell for?" Paige asked as quietly
as she possibly could while still being heard
over the music.

"You'll see," Jasmine replied, smirking.

The rude girl from the bathroom emerged
into the crowd, and Paige suddenly knew she
was the victim. She had pale white hair that
hung down her back, and it perfectly matched
the hair Chloe had used.

"Stumble!" the four girls said in unison.

Instantly the girl tripped over her own two
feet and grabbed a pillar to stop herself from
falling. Paige's eyes widened, alarmed.

"What did that girl do to you?" Paige asked,
glancing at Jasmine.

"She was totally rude on the dance floor earlier. She kept elbowing me. I mean, come on.
This is my dance space, this is your dance space,
right? How hard can it be?" Jasmine glanced at
her friends, and then they all looked at the blond
girl again. She was sidling up next to a tall,
handsome guy in full seductress mode.

"Sneeze!" the four girls said.

Suddenly the blond girl let out a huge sneeze
all over the guy she was trying to impress. He
grimaced and wiped his hand on his pants, then
moved away. The blond girl looked mortified as
Jasmine and her friends laughed it up.

"You guys, stop," Paige said, feeling awful.

"Don't be such a goody-goody," Chloe snapped. "One more, girls."

The blond girl was heading for the dance floor, apparently hoping to lose herself in the crowd. Just as she reached the center of the floor and a big group of swank-looking guys and girls, Jasmine and her friends struck again.

"Fall!" they all said together.

The blond girl tripped and fell flat on her face in the center of the group. It looked pretty painful to Paige, but everyone in a ten-yard radius cracked up laughing. The girl pushed herself to her feet and fled the club, pushing her way through packs of people. She was on the verge of tears.

"That's it, I'm outta here," Paige said, thoroughly disgusted.

She didn't care how rude the girl was to her or to Jasmine. You didn't use your powers to hurt innocent people. Not even the semi-innocent. Paige grabbed her purse, and ignoring Jasmine's protests, she wove her way through the crowd and out the side door. The last thing she wanted to do was encounter the crying girl out front, knowing she may have been able to stop it from happening. All she could think about at that moment was getting back to the camp and forgetting this whole day ever happened.

Outside, Paige found herself in an alleyway.

She glanced around, disoriented, and finally saw cars whizzing by at the end of the alley to her right. Deciding it had to be the Strip, she headed for the traffic. But she hadn't taken one step when she heard a loud screech from behind her. A loud *human* screech.

Paige whirled around and saw two figures struggling at the other end of the alley. She rushed toward them, and as she approached she saw the flash of something metal. Paige's heart hit her throat as everything came into full focus at once. A man was holding a girl from behind with a knife at her neck as he struggled to free her purse from her shoulder.

Without giving it a second thought, Paige thrust out her hand and said, "Knife!" The weapon disappeared in a swirl of white light and reappeared in Paige's hand. Stunned, the assailant loosened his grip on the girl, and the victim took the opportunity to land a swift elbow to his gut. The mugger doubled over as the girl ran past Paige and out toward the Strip. She didn't even seem to notice that Paige was standing there, which was probably best. Then there would be no questions. When the mugger regained his breath, he looked up at Paige, blinked once, and then scrambled out the other end of the alleyway.

"Well, at least the night wasn't a total bust," Paige said to herself.

She dropped the knife into a nearby Dumpster and slapped her hands together, proud of a job well done. Then she turned around and saw Jasmine standing at the side door, her mouth dropped open in awe. Paige froze.

"What the hell was that?" Jasmine asked.

"Any chance you'd believe a trick of light?" Paige asked with a pleading smile.

Jasmine shifted her weight from one leg to the other and crossed her arms over her chest, waiting. She even arched one eyebrow, something Paige had been trying to perfect for years.

"Yeah, didn't think so," Paige said. She was busted, but even worse, her sisters were going to kill her.

Chapter

8

"This is a nightmare," Phoebe said morosely as she, Piper, and Paige dragged their feet along the deserted path to the dining hall the following morning.

After what had happened to each of them the night before, not one of them was in a particular rush to be seen in public. Fortunately the campground was so dead it hardly seemed like a public place. Not only had a lot of people vacated the premises, but the sisters had purposely left their tent late so that they wouldn't bump into Christian or Jasmine on the way to breakfast. They would have to deal with Tessa and Taryn at the table, but they had decided they'd rather do damage control one freaked-out Wiccan at a time.

Phoebe was trying to keep her cool, but it was impossible in the dry heat. It wasn't even ten o'clock, and already it had to be approaching ninety degrees. She was sweating from heat and anxiety and had to keep blotting her face with a tissue.

"It's gonna be okay. I really think it's gonna be okay," Paige said, fiddling with the end of one of her two short braids. Aside from the fidgeting, she looked calm and collected, and Phoebe found herself wishing she'd put her own hair up, too.

"How?" Piper asked, turning to both of them as she paused outside the dining hall. "How it is going to be okay?"

There was a moment of silence, and then Paige sighed. "I have no idea," she replied. "Maybe I can orb us to Alaska?!"

"Oooh! I like that plan!" Phoebe said with a hopeful grin.

Piper groaned and closed her eyes briefly, her hand on the door handle. They all knew that escape was not an option. "What I don't get is how we could both be so stupid as to get caught using our powers on the same night," she said to Paige.

"Yep. You *are* a couple of idiots," Phoebe said, swinging her arms forward and clapping her hands together. Her sisters both gave her the patented Charmed glare. "Sorry. I was just trying to lighten the situation." She cleared her throat, yanked down on the waist of her flowered capris, and slid by Piper.

"I'm going in. Cover me," she said dramatically. Then she walked into the dining hall, head held high, even though she felt more like ducking along the wall.

Everyone in the room looked up when the Charmed Ones arrived, and Phoebe froze, waiting for the questions, the accusations, the awe and fear. But apparently they had looked up only out of run-of-the-mill curiosity, because they instantly went back to their food. That, at least, was a relief. It meant Jasmine, Christian, Tessa, and Taryn hadn't run around the camp the night before spreading the news of the freaks with the crazy powers. Phoebe was actually kind of impressed.

The atmosphere in the dining hall was completely different than it had been the day before. Gone was the laughter; the loud, raucous conversation; the din worthy of a Super Bowl game. Half the tables were empty, and the other half were occupied by whispering groups of people bent over their plates. None of the covens were looking at anyone beyond their own tables, and the air was so thick with paranoia Phoebe could practically taste it.

Swallowing back her nervousness, Phoebe looked over at table 3 and found that Tessa and Taryn were waiting for them expectantly— along with Christian and Jasmine. They all exchanged looks after Phoebe noticed them, and it was perfectly clear that Jasmine had compared notes with the others. They knew that both Piper and Paige had powers and probably figured Phoebe did as well, by association.

"Looks like we have a couple of defectors at our table," Phoebe said under her breath, running her hand along the back of her neck.

"Why don't I just orb to McDonald's, get us some breakfast, and meet you back at the tent?" Paige suggested, bouncing on the balls of her feet. "Or better yet, what about those buffets we saw as we drove in? All you can eat?" she prodded, waggling her eyebrows.

"Come on, Paige, we're gonna have to deal with them sometime," Piper said, linking her arm with her sister's and starting down the center aisle. "Remember what we talked about last night. We all just say as little as humanly possible."

Phoebe fell into step behind Piper and Paige as they approached table 3. When they arrived at the end of the table, four pairs of eyes looked up at them expectantly. They looked like little kids at story time. Phoebe grinned her brightest grin.

"Hey, everyone!" she said. "Oh, good! Pancakes!"

She slipped by Christian and Jasmine, sat down, and started slapping food onto her plate. Piper and Paige followed Phoebe's lead and did the same. Phoebe didn't think for a minute that the other Wiccans were going to let them get away without saying anything, but she was hoping to put it off for as long as possible. After a couple of minutes of silence, however, Phoebe could no longer take the feeling of everyone staring at her. She finally made eye contact with Taryn across the table.

"So, what are you guys?" Taryn asked bluntly. Phoebe didn't even know the girl had it in her to say something so tactlessly direct and almost mean. But the question had clearly taken a lot out of Taryn. Her face was all pink from the exertion, as if she'd been gathering her courage to say it for a long time.

"Taryn!" Tessa gasped, touching her sister's arm. "What kind of question is that?"

"A legitimate one, I'd say," Christian put in, turning to Phoebe with his big brown eyes. "Care to answer it?"

"Well, we're Wiccans, just like you guys," Phoebe said nonchalantly. She busied herself dousing her pancakes with syrup.

"Right, just like us," Jasmine said, her black curls bouncing as she nodded sarcastically. "Even *I* don't have powers like you guys do, and I've been practicing since, like, *birth*. My mother was a very powerful Wiccan," she explained to the others matter-of-factly.

"Would you mind keeping your voice down?" Piper asked through her teeth, leaning in close to the table. "The last thing we need is for someone to overhear you talking about our powers," she whispered.

"Why?" Christian asked. He sat up straight, resting his elbows on the table, and eyed Piper suspiciously. Phoebe couldn't help noticing the fact that he was flexing his impressive biceps under his T-shirt, trying to be menacing. "Why wouldn't you want everyone to know what you can do?" he added.

"Because we'd rather not have *everyone* in this place sitting at our table tomorrow morning looking at us like you are right now," Piper shot back.

The others fell silent for a moment, and everyone looked down at their untouched breakfasts. Phoebe wracked her brain for something to say that would explain away what these people had witnessed, but they weren't stupid. They knew that Piper's freezing ability and Paige's orbing ability weren't normal Wiccan powers. The feats the Charmed Ones could perform went way beyond the voodoo-doll mojo Paige had watched Jasmine and her friends put on some girl last night.

"Look, you guys," Paige said finally. Phoebe held her breath, just hoping her little sister wasn't about to heedlessly spill every last bean. She loved Paige, but the girl did have a small issue with speaking before she thought.

"Let's just say we've honed our power a little

more, okay?" Paige said. "We're very dedicated to our craft. It's pretty much all we do."

Everyone seemed to absorb this, and for a moment Phoebe thought they were just going to accept it. Score one for Paige. But then everyone spoke at once.

"But freezing time isn't exactly a small—"

"I'm sorry, but I just can't believe what I saw was—"

"You can't just mess with people like—"

Phoebe's head was about to hit the table in sheer desperation, when suddenly a loud male voice sliced through the conversation and everyone in the dining hall fell silent. Dead silent.

"Everyone! We found Craig."

It was Damon, the African-American guy who had first made the announcement the morning before. But today he wasn't so wild eyed. Today he was absolutely morose. And this time no one had heard him come in. Christian stood the moment the words were out of Damon's mouth.

"He's dead, Christian," Damon said, looking him right in the eye from across the room. "Craig is dead."

"I can't believe this," Piper said, glancing around the basement room she and half the population of the camp were gathered in. "All these people shouldn't be here."

"It wasn't like we were going to be able to

stop them," Paige said. "They have a right to know what's going on."

"Yeah, but they're compromising the crime scene," Piper said through her teeth.

"Someone's been spending too much time around Daryl," Phoebe quipped.

Everyone hovered outside the door to the storage closet in which Craig's body had been found—everyone who hadn't been scared away by the finding of an actual corpse. Marcia Farina was in hysterics in the far corner, being comforted by a few women who apparently came to the Gathering every year. Ryan Treetop leaned against the wall next to her, his head bowed, his face turned away from Piper and her sisters.

Apparently Treetop had remembered the old storage closet this morning, housed in the basement under his office. He said that no one had been down there for years—a story that was supported by the fact that there was about an inch of dust and grime on everything in the room. He didn't think that anyone else even new it existed. That morning he and Marcia had gone to check it out, just in case, hoping and assuming they would find nothing. Minutes later Treetop had arrived at the door to Damon's tent, looking as grim as death itself.

Piper looked up as Christian emerged from the room. He appeared frail, as if he could barely hold himself up, and his soulful eyes had gone flat. Piper clutched her elbows. Whatever he'd seen in there had taken a lot out of him. He started past her and her sisters without even seeing them.

"Christian," Piper whispered. He turned slowly and tried to focus on her. His skin looked green in the dim light of the basement. "Can we inspect the body before the police get here?"

"Sure," he said, half dazed, lifting his hand toward the door. "I don't know if you want to. . . ." He practically fell into the arms of two of his brethren as he walked away, and they helped him up the rickety stairs. Piper's heart went out to him, but she didn't want to waste any time. She and her sisters turned and slipped into the storage room.

"Oh, my God," Phoebe said as Paige closed the door behind them. Piper covered her nose and mouth to keep from retching. Craig's body, lit by the light from a single swinging bulb overhead, was dressed in boxer shorts and a T-shirt. He was propped up against the wall in a seated position, but all his limbs were limp—more limp than they should have been. His skin sagged from his bones, and there was no color in his body at all. He was sheer white—as if he'd been frozen. Or scared out of his mind. Or . . .

"I think something took all his blood," Paige said, crouching next to the body on the dirt-covered cement floor, but being careful not to touch Craig. "Vampire?" she asked, looking up at her sisters.

"I don't think so," Piper said, crouching across from Paige. She pointed at a nasty puncture wound in Craig's arm, just at the bend of his elbow.

Paige looked down at the arm next to her and found another. "Eeeeehh," she said, scrunching up her nose.

"You guys, there are two more above his knees," Phoebe put in, kneeling next to Paige.

"Not a vampire, then," Piper said, standing and slapping her dirty hands together. "They traditionally suck from the neck. They don't systematically drain blood through the major veins like doctors."

Phoebe started to stand, lost her balance, and flung her hand out to steady herself. Instead of grabbing the floor, her hand hit Craig's leg, and she froze, her eyes squeezing shut. At first Piper thought she was just freaked out over having touched the dead body, but then she realized her sister was having a vision. Paige pushed herself up and took a step toward Piper. They both watched Phoebe and waited.

"Ugh!" Phoebe said suddenly, jumping up and away from the body. She wiped her hands on her thighs and looked at her sisters shakily.

"What did you see?" Piper asked, almost afraid to know.

"They drained his blood with these long needles," Phoebe said, swallowing with difficulty. "It was definitely those jackal things. And I saw them going back to some kind of ritual chamber, but guys . . . this is really weird . . . I swear they were in an elevator."

"They're staying in a *hotel*?" Paige asked.

"In the penthouse, I think," Phoebe said skeptically. "The little *P* button was lit up in the elevator."

"Well, if I ran a hotel, that's where I'd put the bloodsucking demons. In the penthouse," Piper said dryly.

"I know it sounds weird, but when was the last time my visions were wrong?" Phoebe said.

"Try never," Paige replied. "We have to talk to Leo. Let's go back to the tent and call him."

The sisters left the room and found that most of the other Wiccans had already cleared out. As they went upstairs the police were coming down, asking if anyone had touched the body or compromised the scene. Piper, Paige, and Phoebe slipped by quickly and hurried back to their tent. The moment they were inside, they all called out together.

"Leo!"

He appeared instantly with Cole by his side. "We were just coming to see you," Leo said. "I think Cole may have found your demons in the Book of Shadows."

Phoebe rushed over to Cole and wrapped her arms around him, closing her eyes happily. He was wearing a dark blue suit with a lighter blue shirt and tie underneath, as if he'd just come from an interview, and he looked a bit worn out. His expression lightened considerably, however, when he found Phoebe in his arms.

"I wasn't expecting you," she said with a smile.

"I wanted to see how you were doing," he said, kissing her forehead. He held her face in both hands and tilted her head so she was looking up at him. "Everything okay?"

"Not exactly," Phoebe replied with a sigh. "We just found out our demons are the bloodsucking type."

"But not vampires," Paige put in. "Phoebe had a vision, and they used needles."

"And they've stepped it up from kidnapping to killing," Piper said, cupping her forehead with her hand. "Although I guess that means that all the other victims are probably dead. . . ."

Piper felt her stomach turn as she thought of Tessa and Taryn and what they must be going through now that one of the victims had been found dead. She wanted to cry for them, but she couldn't. She didn't have time. She had to find the demons that had done this and make them pay.

"You can't assume that yet," Leo told her, gently pushing her long hair behind her shoulder.

"Well, what did you find?" Phoebe asked, clearly ready to get down to business just like Piper.

"The bloodsucking fits into our theory, so I think we have your men, in a manner of speaking," Leo said. "Paige, maybe you should orb the book here, just for a couple of minutes, so you can read what we found."

Paige looked at her sisters uncertainly. She had learned early on in her days as a Charmed One that the Book of Shadows was not supposed to leave the manor. But Piper nodded her approval. "It's all right," she said. "We need it right about now."

Closing her eyes, Paige held out her hands, concentrated for a moment, and said, "Book of Shadows." A dazzling white light swirled to life in her hands, and the huge family tome appeared, already open to the page in question.

Piper, Phoebe, Cole, and Leo gathered around Paige, reading over her shoulders. Piper instantly recognized the drawing. It was a perfect likeness of the jackal-faced creature from the videotape she and Phoebe had seen the night before. A thrill of fear washed down her spine, and she rolled her shoulders back, staving it off. Whatever it was, she and her sisters would face it and bring it down.

"'Anubi,'" Piper read from across the top of the page. She took the large book from Paige's hands, and the spine creaked and cracked as she sat down on her cot. Leo sat next to her, and Paige crawled onto the mattress behind them, while Phoebe and Cole waited in the center of the room.

"'The first records of the Anubi originated in ancient Egypt in the Nile Delta,'" Piper read aloud. "'They were demigods, followers of the god Anubis, who decided the fate of the soul upon death. After betraying Anubis, the Anubi were cast off to live a mortal life and to die a mortal death.'"

Piper paused and looked up at Cole. "So if they became mortal thousands of years ago, why were they walking around twenty-first century Vegas a couple of nights ago? Shouldn't they be major dust piles by now?"

"Keep reading," Cole instructed, pulling at the knot in his tie. He freed himself from it and tossed it on Phoebe's bed, then undid his top button.

Piper took a deep breath and looked down at the book again. "'Decades after their banishment, as the Anubi began to grow weak, they went to a witch to demand a spell that would return them to demigods before their imminent death. When the witch couldn't help them, they killed her and drank her blood. It is in this way they discovered that they gained strength from the blood of witches. That they could, in fact, live forever off their blood.'"

"Okay, this is starting to make more sense," Paige said, sitting back. "Icky sense, but sense."

Piper scanned the rest of the page. "It says they drain the blood and keep it in canisters to be stored and used later. They need to drink only a bit at a time, but apparently they're plan-for-the-future demons."

"Is there a vanquishing spell?" Phoebe asked, pacing the room. "Just tell me there's a vanquishing spell so we can annihilate these things."

Piper flipped the page. "Bingo, baby!" she said, slapping the book with the back of her hand. "It says they can be vanquished by a simple Power of Three spell."

"Ah! That's what I like to hear," Phoebe said with a smile. "Now all we have to do is figure out what hotel they're staying in and find the little suckers." She scrunched up her face apologetically. "Uh, no pun intended. Sorry."

"Wait a minute, they're staying in a hotel?" Cole asked.

"According to my vision," Phoebe replied.

Piper closed the book and handed it to Leo. "Okay, you're a really old Egyptian demon, you come to Vegas—"

"Which they probably love, considering the climate around here," Phoebe said, lifting her hair off her neck and fanning herself with her hand.

"It's just like home to them," Cole agreed, shrugging out of his jacket, as if to accentuate the point.

"So, they're here for a little gambling, a little comedy, a little bloodletting," Paige continued. "Where do they set up shop?"

"Omigod, you guys! I've got it!" Phoebe exclaimed. "Isn't there a pyramid casino? You know, the one with that huge light beam thing coming out the top?!"

"The Luxor!" Paige said, her eyes lighting up as she pushed herself off the cot. She grabbed her tourist map of the Strip out of the side pocket on her bag and flattened it on the table. "It's down here at the end," she said, pointing to the hotel. "You know, the Anubi probably get some of their strength from that whole pyramid power thing. And I bet they can walk right through the lobby without drawing much attention. People probably think they're part of the theme. Why didn't we think of this before?"

"Well, we thought of it now," Piper said, grabbing the map. Her adrenaline was already pumping, and she couldn't wait to find these things and get this whole ordeal over with. "Come on. Let's go vanquish some demons."

The servant entered its master's chamber, its black robes swishing as it walked. The walls were lined with black candles, flickering and dancing as the servant passed them by. The Great One knelt before the bloodstained altar, eyes closed, palms turned up in supplication. The servant stood behind its master in patient silence, as it had been trained to do.

"You come to disturb my meditation with ill tidings?" the Great One asked, body rigid.

"Never, Your Grace," the servant replied with a bow. "Only to bring you joyous news."

The Great One lowered its hands and stood slowly, pulling its hood away from its face as it turned. Its eyes were thick with pure, unadulterated evil. It cocked its head, intrigued.

"Speak," it commanded.

"It is confirmed, O Great One." The servant bowed once more, clasping its hands together. "They exist. And they are here."

"The Charmed Ones," the Great One breathed.

Another bow. The servant continued. "Their power is even greater than we imagined, Your Grace. If we can capture them, our circle will be complete. Our ascension to power a definite. Their blood is pure and strong. It is all we need to finish this. To become that which we were meant to be."

"You use the word *if*. Do you have some reason to believe that we will not prevail over these . . . *girls*?" the Great One demanded with a sneer.

"No, Your Grace," the servant answered

quickly, sensing there could be no other answer without a violent reaction. "Yes, they are powerful, but they are, at the moment, distracted. They are too trusting, too . . . innocent."

"Then, it will be simple for us to take them," the Great One said, lifting the hood again. It turned and lowered itself to its knees at the altar once more, raising its hands and tilting its head to the sky. "It will be as simple as one . . . two . . . three. . . ."

Chapter
9

Piper led the way out of the tent and headed for the parking lot near the front of the camp. All she could think about was getting to the Luxor and what they were going to do once they got there. They couldn't exactly walk up to the front desk and ask if they had a bunch of demons staying there. If the Anubi were holed up in the hotel somewhere, the people that worked there probably didn't know about it. If they did, they would have contacted the *National Enquirer* by now.

"Piper!" Leo called out, jogging to catch up with her. "Where are we going?" he asked. He had already orbed the Book of Shadows back to the manor but had opted to come back and help them just in case they ran into trouble at the Luxor. He skidded up next to her and grabbed her upper arm, forcing her to stop.

Piper swung around, slightly out of breath from rushing in the heat. Her hair fanned out as she spun, generating a pleasant little breeze that cooled her off for about two seconds.

"I'm going to the car, Leo, where do you think I'm going?" she said.

"Why don't we just orb there? Time being of the essence, I mean," Leo suggested, glancing around to make sure no one was in earshot, just as Paige walked up to join them. Phoebe and Cole were bringing up the rear, Phoebe already scribbling on her notepad.

"Yeah, Piper," Paige said. "May as well use what we got."

"You guys, we don't know where in the hotel the Anubi are, or if they're even there," Piper said patiently. "We can't have you orbing us into some tourist's room or right into the middle of the casino. Besides, Phoebe needs time to work on a spell. She can do it in the car."

"Oh," Leo said, glancing sheepishly at Paige. "Good point."

"There's a reason she's the oldest," Paige said with only a trace of sarcasm.

"Let's go," Piper said, scrounging through her bag for the keys to the convertible.

At this point the formerly packed parking lot was almost empty. It was depressing to see the place so deserted. As much as Piper had picked on the people that had been there, the lovefest party atmosphere had been kind of cool. Now the Wiccans were being scared off in droves. Piper just hoped that in a little while none of them would have to be scared anymore.

She unlocked the car and tossed her bag on the floor. Phoebe, Cole, and Paige climbed into the backseat, and Leo was just opening the door to the passenger side when Piper heard footsteps crunching through the dirt and gravel. She turned to find Christian and Jasmine jogging up to them, both gasping for breath.

"Great," Piper said through her teeth. "Just what we need."

"Where're you guys going?" Jasmine asked, holding her stomach as her breathing slowly returned to normal. She was wearing a black T-shirt, a black skirt, black tights, and huge black boots. Piper had no idea how she was able to stand the heat in her outfit, but apparently she was a style-before-comfort kind of girl.

"Are you on a mission or something?" Jasmine added, sounding a little too interested for Piper's comfort. "Are you going to use your powers again?"

Piper glanced at her sisters, and they stared back at her blankly, as did Cole. Leo cleared his throat and looked away, taking sudden great interest in the landmarkless desert skyline. Apparently it was Piper's turn to come up with a cover story. She'd have to check the rotation on that one.

"Actually, we're just going to . . . see the tigers!" Piper said brightly. "So, see ya!"

"The tigers?" Christian asked skeptically, hands on hips. He seemed to have gathered himself together since the last time she saw him. Piper almost preferred the dazed, question-free Christian. "First you want to see Craig's body, and now you're going to look at tigers?"

Piper plopped down behind the wheel, turned, and shot Paige a *help me* look.

"Yeah, you know, at the Mirage!" Paige said. "I find wild animals very soothing to the nerves. We'd ask you to come, but there's no more room in the car." She batted her eyelashes innocently, and Piper hoped for the best.

"Look, if you guys have a lead on whoever killed Craig, I want to come with you," Christian said, leaning on the back of the car. "You can't just leave me out of it."

"Christian . . . ," Piper began.

But before she could even formulate a sentence, Jasmine stepped up next to Leo and rested her hand on his arm, looking up at him appreciatively. Leo shot Piper an almost frightened glance as Jasmine actually squeezed his biceps.

"Where did you come from?" Jasmine asked, raising her eyebrows as she tossed her curls flirtatiously. "Do you have special powers, too?"

"All right, that's it," Piper said. "Leo, sit."

He quickly sat down in the passenger seat and closed the door. Then, before Christian and Jasmine could even breathe, she froze them right on the spot.

"You didn't have to do that, Piper," Paige admonished.

"Oh, yes I did," Piper said. She started the car and peeled out. Just before she hit the driveway, she flicked her hand back in Jasmine and Christian's direction, unfreezing them so no one would find them in suspended animation.

"Hey!" Jasmine shouted seconds later, after she'd recovered herself. "You can't do that to us! Get back here!"

Piper tried not to laugh. *That's what you get for messing with my man.*

And, of course, for hindering the work of the Charmed Ones.

The moment Piper walked into the Luxor, she was struck with an overwhelming sense of awe. The place was *huge*! She hoped Phoebe was right about the Anubi being in the penthouse, because if they were hiding somewhere else in this monstrous building, it was going to take forever to find them. And Piper didn't have forever. Some of the kidnapping victims could potentially still be alive, but the longer it took for her and her sisters to find them, the smaller the chances were for the missing Wiccans.

"Where the heck are the elevators?" Phoebe said, standing next to Piper as she took in her surroundings with wide eyes.

There were people everywhere, standing at the check-in desk, loitering in the lobby, crossing through to the casino, which was down a few steps from where Piper stood. The standard casino noises—bells dinging, men cheering, change falling into trays—filled the air. The hotel decor itself contributed to the busyness. Everywhere Piper looked there was another sphinx or golden statue, and she could have gone cross-eyed from the labyrinthine patterns on the carpeting and wallpaper.

"You guys! Over there!" Paige said, pointing at a tiny gold sign with an arrow pointing toward the elevators. "They must be down that hall."

"Okay. Let's do this," Piper said.

As they turned toward the elevators she swore she heard someone calling her name. She decided it had to be a trick of the ear. With all the noises in this place, her head was probably just messing with her. Then, however, she felt a hand on her back and whirled around. Her heart instantly leaped into her throat. Taryn and Tessa were standing right in front of her.

"Hey," Tessa said, taking a deep breath. "Sorry if I startled you."

Tessa's short hair was pushed back in a headband, and both she and Taryn were wearing head-to-toe black. They looked like either cat burglars or supermodels, with their modern blond haircuts and their sleek outfits. Of course, they probably weren't trying to be sleek, Piper realized. They were probably wearing black as a sign of mourning, now that they knew their sister was most likely gone forever.

"What are you guys doing here?" Piper asked, pushing her hair behind her ear.

"Well, we followed you," Tessa said, smiling apologetically. "We know that Christian let you see the body, and we figured you may have found something out about, you know, what might have happened to Tina."

Piper's heart squeezed painfully, and she looked at her sisters. How was she supposed to break the news to these girls that their sister had most likely died in a painful and heinous way, that she had been drained by a bunch of demons? Was that something they could even wrap their brains around—the existence of actual demons?

"Look, Piper," Taryn chimed in. Piper snapped back to attention at the surprising sound of Taryn's voice. "We realize that Tina is probably dead, and we'll have to deal with that. But if you're going after her killer, we want to come. I want to see the person who did this to her. To us."

The expression in her steel blue eyes was so

determined Piper couldn't even think of turning her down. She looked at her sisters and knew that they were thinking the same thing. It was time to let Tessa and Taryn in on a few little secrets. But revealing those secrets was going to mean a lot of explanation.

"All right, but I have to warn you, we may not actually be dealing with a person here," Piper said quietly, leading the group over to the nearest wall.

"Come again?" Tessa asked, raising her eyebrows.

"It's hard to explain, but basically, demons are real, and we think that a few of them may be responsible for the kidnappings," Phoebe said. "And for Craig's death."

"Demons are real," Taryn repeated flatly. Piper held her breath as Taryn and Tessa glanced at each other skeptically. Then Taryn looked Piper right in the eye, her expression determined, her jaw set. "All right, then. Let's go find these demons."

Piper almost smiled, impressed with how easily they accepted Phoebe's brief explanation. That took a certain degree of open-mindedness that she almost never came across. But at the same time her mind was shouting a thousand protests. They could not lead these innocents into a battle. They couldn't put more people in danger just because they *wanted* to come. But she also couldn't ignore their plea. She knew that if something had taken Paige or Phoebe, she'd want to face it down herself. She knew that nothing would be able to stop her from doing just that.

"All right," Piper said finally, turning and heading for the gold elevators. "But you have to stay back once we find these things. We don't know what's going to happen."

"Fine," Tessa said, falling in step with her. "No problem."

Piper hit the Up button for the elevator and stepped back to wait, purposely avoiding eye contact with both Leo and Cole. She knew that they didn't approve of her allowing Tessa and Taryn to come, but it was too late now.

"I don't think this is such a good idea," Cole said quietly, stepping up next to Piper in front of the elevator doors. "How are you going to concentrate on vanquishing these things while you have to protect those two?"

"Cole, this is important to them," Piper said under her breath. She looked up at Leo. "If things get hairy up there, I want you to grab them and orb them out of there, okay?"

"Okay," Leo said reluctantly.

The elevator let out a loud ding and the doors slid open. Piper and the others stepped in, Phoebe clutching her vanquishing spell.

"Well," Piper said, hitting the penthouse button. "Here goes nothing."

• • •

"This has to be it," Phoebe said the moment she stepped out of the elevator on the top floor. There were only two doors along the short hallway, one to the left marked P1 and one to the right marked P2. "It's too quiet up here. And way too hot."

Piper swallowed back her trepidation as she walked along the hall behind her sister. The lights along the walls had been dimmed and the air-conditioning to the floor had been cut off, making the air almost unbearable. Piper made herself breathe shallowly as they crept across the plush carpet.

"Hold on a sec," Paige whispered, stopping in her tracks. "You guys hear that?"

Everyone froze, and Piper trained her ear on the door to her left. It took a few seconds, but then she heard it. A low, ritual mumbling. The depth of the voices gave her chills all the way to the bottoms of her feet. It felt as if the voices were rumbling through her heart and lungs.

"This has to be it," she whispered, feeling the sudden rush of adrenaline she always felt when she and her sisters were about to go into battle. She looked at Tessa and Taryn, both of whom were as white as ghosts. "Stay behind us, you got it?"

They both nodded mutely, and Piper couldn't even tell if they were still breathing. They were clearly petrified, and for the fiftieth time in the last two minutes she rethought her decision to let them come. But there was no going back now.

"Okay, on the count of three," Piper said, her hand on the doorknob. "One . . . two . . . three!"

She threw open the door, intending to freeze the room and get a moment to assess the situation, but the second she saw the Anubi, she froze in fear. There were three of them, just like in the video, but they were each at least ten feet tall. They loomed above her, practically filling the room. Painted on the floor was a pyramid inside a circle, and the Anubi stood around the symbol. All the furniture had been moved against the walls, and the paintings had been removed and replaced by masks of Egyptian gods. The moment Piper opened the door, all three huge, monstrous jackal faces turned to glare at the intruders.

"Who dares enter here?" one of the Anubi growled in an unearthly, rumbling voice. Its eyes flashed red, and it extended its arm like a weapon. Piper braced herself for a blast, but before the monster could unleash whatever powers it had, Phoebe launched herself into the air, hovering for a moment before landing a powerful kick across the Anubi's snout. The demon's head tipped to the side, but otherwise it barely moved.

Phoebe came down to the floor again, gripping her foot in pain.

"Phoebe!" Cole shouted, rushing to her side.

"Okay, hard faces," Phoebe said, looking across the room at her sisters. "Really hard faces."

"So that's what you can do!" Tessa exclaimed in wonder, as if she'd momentarily forgotten that they were all in some serious peril. "You can fly."

"Not exactly, but that's not the point to focus on at the moment," Paige said as the Anubi started to advance on them. "Phoebe! The spell!"

Cole pulled Phoebe to her feet, and she started toward Piper and Paige, but suddenly one of the Anubi backhanded her across the face and she went tumbling head over heels into a corner. She crumpled to the ground, limp, and one of the gold masks that decorated the walls fell on top of her. Cole let out a guttural growl and threw a punch at the Anubi, but it tossed him as well. Piper's first instinct was to run to Phoebe and Cole, but the Anubi blocked her way. Out of the corner of her eye she saw Leo hustle Taryn and Tessa into the far corner and stand in front of them, shielding them from whatever was to come. Meanwhile, Cole crawled over to Phoebe and tried to rouse her.

Suddenly one of the Anubi turned on Paige and lifted its palm. A gleaming orange energy ball appeared, hovering in front of its hand. The creature pushed it in Paige's direction, and it went hurtling through the air, aimed at her head.

Paige squealed and was instantly enveloped in her own white light. The energy ball went right through the space where she had been and exploded against the wall, shattering a mirror and burning a hole in the wallpaper.

Piper heard Tessa shriek and saw that she, Taryn, and Leo had all been hit by the flying glass. They had little cuts and scratches all over their faces and hands.

"Leo," Piper said. "It just got too dangerous in here."

"Got it," he replied.

He orbed himself and the sisters out of the room, even as Taryn and Tessa protested that they wanted to stay. Piper had to admire their determination. At this point she would get out of here if she could. At least Tessa and Taryn were safe now. Leo would heal their cuts and keep them out of harm's way.

Suddenly Paige reappeared on the other side of the room, and the Anubi reeled on her, their eyes now burning brightly in their evil faces.

"Witch!" they all exclaimed at once, their voices rocking the room.

"Okay, they sound excited now," Paige said, terrified.

One of the Anubi pulled a long, sharp needle out of its robes and advanced on Paige. Another produced a gleaming gold canister. Piper's heart sickened when she realized what they were about to do. Paige whimpered and shrank back against the wall just as Phoebe blinked her eyes open, slowly coming to in Cole's arms.

"Piper!" Phoebe shouted. "Do something!"

Piper did the only thing she could. She flung her hands out in the direction of the threatening Anubi, and it instantly exploded and disappeared in a flash of fiery light. Paige cried out and covered her face against the heat and intense light of the explosion. But it was gone in an instant, leaving nothing but a singed smell in the air. For a moment no one in the room moved. Then the remaining two Anubi looked at Piper, clearly stunned.

"You'll pay for that, witch," one of them said.

"Not likely," Piper replied, excited. "Looks like we won't need the vanquishing spell after all, Phoebe." She flung out her hands again and destroyed the second Anubi, causing the third to let out an unholy screech of mind-bending volume. Piper was about to dust the third demon, when Phoebe launched herself up from the floor and caught Piper's arm.

"Uh-uh. This one we need for questioning," Phoebe said.

The door behind Piper was thrown open, and Leo, Tessa, and Taryn came in, looking wildly around the room.

"What was that?" Leo asked.

"That was the sound of a demon realizing it

was all alone in the world," Piper replied.

"Say your prayers, witch," the third Anubi said to Piper.

"These guys sure love the catch phrases," Paige said under her breath.

The Anubi pulled its arm back, and an energy ball appeared in its hand. Paige shouted out "Energy ball!" and suddenly the fiery orb was in *her* hand. The Anubi screeched again, looking around in confusion, and Phoebe used the moment of surprise to land a solid roundhouse kick in the Anubi's gut area. She winced as her leg landed, but the Anubi doubled over. Then Piper watched in surprise as Phoebe rushed the creature with all her might and basically wrestled it to the ground.

"Nice tackle," Piper said.

"It was the only thing I could think to do," Phoebe replied, struggling to hold the thing down. "Uh, guys?" she said, looking to Cole and Leo for help.

They both hit the floor, and together the three of them managed to pin the Anubi to the ground. It bucked and writhed under their grip, but Paige sauntered over and held its own ball of fire over its face menacingly.

"Oh, no. You're not going anywhere," Paige said. "Not until you tell us what you've done with all the witches you've taken."

The Anubi let out a low, menacing laugh, and

a chill ran down Piper's spine. "They're all dead," it told them. "But we still have their blood, if you're interested."

Piper's breath caught in her throat as the Anubi turned its massive head toward a line of more than twenty canisters on the windowsill. If each one held the blood of a different witch, then there were even more victims than they had thought. Suddenly Piper felt her whole body go numb. She turned and looked at Tessa and Taryn, who were huddled together by the door.

"That means Tina is . . . Tina is actually . . ." Taryn took one step away from her sister and fainted, her body falling limp on the floor. Tessa crumbled next to her, rested her face on her sister's arm, and started to sob.

Her heart twisting painfully, Piper turned slowly back to the Anubi, lifted her hands, and just as Phoebe, Cole, and Leo flung themselves out of harm's way, blew it to pieces.

Chapter

10

By the time Piper, Phoebe, Paige, Taryn, and Tessa returned to the campground, Piper felt as if she'd fought ten rounds in the ring with ten demons. She was exhausted from the fight, but also from the turmoil of the last few days. She had used a pay phone to call the police from the lobby of the Luxor and anonymously tip them that the Wiccans' kidnappers had been found. Piper was certain that the blood they found in those canisters would match the blood types of the missing Wiccans. What she couldn't imagine was the reaction the police were going to have to the bizarre crime scene and the lack of human fingerprints.

Everyone was silent in the car on the way back. The quiet was punctuated only by the random sobs from Taryn and Tessa, who were cuddled together in the backseat next to a bruised and tired Phoebe.

As Piper pulled by the cop cars parked at the edge of the campground's drive she noticed the two policemen were talking furiously into their radios.

"They're getting the news now," Piper said, resting her elbow on top of the door and her head in her hand.

"At least that's over with," Paige replied.

Piper sighed sadly as she pulled the car into the parking lot. Leo had already orbed himself and Cole back home to check on the manor before giving the news of their vanquishings to the Elders. As Piper parked and pushed herself out of her seat she found herself wishing Leo hadn't left so quickly. She could definitely go for a nice, comforting hug right about now.

Phoebe and Paige climbed out of the car, but Tessa and Taryn made no sign of moving. Tessa had her arms around Taryn's small form, and both of them had their eyes closed. Piper shared a look of sympathy with her sisters. She had no problem imagining the pain Tessa and Taryn were feeling at that moment.

"You guys . . . we're back," she said quietly. "You can stay here if you want. . . ."

"No, that's okay," Tessa said, sitting up straight and sniffling. "We're gonna have to get out of your car sometime."

She pushed herself across the seat and climbed shakily out, then turned to help her sister out as well. Taryn moved as if her body were now made of sand. Every movement seemed to take great effort, and her limbs hung like dead weight. Piper wondered if the poor girl would ever be herself again.

"Wow. This place is barren," Tessa said, squinting her puffy red eyes slightly as she looked around. There was only a handful of cars in the parking lot now, and the sky was starting to cloud over. The wind was picking up as well, but it had lost its thick, hot feeling. There was even a slight chill in the air.

"Well, we may as well go find whoever's left and tell them the good news," Paige said. Then she looked at Tessa and Taryn, and a mortified blush darkened her face. "I mean, that there won't be any more kidnappings," she added quickly. "Not that—"

"We know what you meant, Paige," Tessa said, wrapping her arm around Taryn's shoulders. "It's okay."

Paige smiled apologetically, and Piper wrapped her arms around her sister's back.

"Actually, I think we'd better let the police tell them," Piper said, rubbing Paige's back. "If we do it, there are going to be too many questions."

"Good point," Paige said.

"Speaking of which," Phoebe began slowly, looking at Tessa and Taryn, "it might be better if you guys didn't tell anyone what you saw today. Ever."

"Your secret's safe with us," Tessa said as Taryn rested her head on her sister's shoulder. "If it weren't for you guys, we might never have found out what happened to Tina. Now that we know, maybe we can start to move on."

Piper reached out and squeezed Tessa's hand, and the little group walked toward the dining hall. Ever since Craig had been found that morning, the building had become like Crisis Central. The covens had been gathering there for a mixture of protection and support, not wanting to be left alone in their tents. When Phoebe pulled the door open, about thirty faces turned to look at her, startled. Jasmine's coven was seated at the nearest table, fiddling with tarot cards; Christian's coven sat a few tables down; and the women who had worn the white dresses for the meet-and-greet were present as well. Marcia Farina sat with them, sipping something from a steaming cup and looking quite pale.

Piper led everyone over to the nearest table and sat down. Phoebe and Paige took the two chairs next to her, and Tessa and Taryn slumped down across from them. None of them were surprised when Christian and Jasmine made a beeline for their table from across the room. But when they were only halfway there, the door opened once again.

A slim, young police officer walked in and cleared his throat uncertainly. Everyone in the room dropped what they were doing and turned to look at him. A mixture of fear and hope filled the air.

"Well, it looks like they've found the kidnappers," he said, his eyes flicking around the room without resting on one person for more than a split second. "We received an anonymous tip, and when our investigators went to the designated location, they found two more bodies."

At this he glanced at Christian, who stood in the center aisle, with Jasmine a few feet ahead of him. "Apparently they were in the same condition as your friend," the officer said.

"Did they catch the guys who did it?" Christian asked.

"They have reason to believe the culprits are dead," the officer answered, taking a step back toward the door. "That's all the information I can give you at this time."

"That's bull!" Christian shouted, the veins in his forehead bulging. "What does that mean, 'reason to believe'?" he repeated snidely. "I want to know—"

"Christian!" Phoebe said loudly and firmly, cutting him off. "Calm down." She gazed at him meaningfully, and he seemed to understand that she had something to tell him. He tucked his chin and took a deep breath.

"Sorry, Officer," Christian said. "I guess I'm just a little worked up."

"Don't worry about it. It's understandable," the officer replied, looking relieved that the prospect of confrontation had been averted. "But the chief asked me to tell you all that he believes you're out of danger."

A collective sigh went out across the room, and Piper saw Marcia rest her head on her arms, spent.

"See? Now we can all relax," Ryan Treetop said from his usual spot in the corner. "Everyone can relax and have a good time."

The moment the officer was safely out the door, Christian and Jasmine arrived at the end of the table.

"First of all, you can't just freeze people like that and get away with it," Jasmine said through her teeth.

"Forget about that," Christian said, still seething. "What did you guys do when you left here?"

"We took care of the murderers," Piper answered bluntly. "You can thank us now." She placed her hands flat on the table and stood up, intending to brush right past him. The last thing she wanted to deal with right now was a grand

inquisition. She and her sisters had just vanquished yet another set of demons, making the
world safe for Wiccan-kind, and this guy wanted
to harass her about it.

"Well, who was it?" Christian asked, stepping
in front of Piper and blocking her way.

Phoebe and Paige stood up behind her. Piper
was glad to have their strength at her back.

"Look, if we tell you the truth, you're not
gonna believe us, so will you just accept the fact
that the guys who killed Craig and a lot of other
people are dead, and let it be?" Piper asked.

"So . . . all of the other kidnapping victims . . .
they're all dead?" Jasmine asked, scrunching her
face up uncertainly.

Piper was suddenly hyperaware of the two
sisters across the table who were somehow, by
some miracle, holding it all together in front of
these two emotionless morons.

"It looks that way," Piper said quietly. Then
she trained her best glare on Christian. "Now,
we'd really like to go back to our tent, if you
would please get out of the way."

"Not until you—"

"Christian, come on, we've all had a long
day," Tessa said suddenly, sounding exhausted.
"We'll explain later."

Everyone turned to look at her, surprised that
she felt the need to get involved in this, with
everything that she was going through. But her

plea seemed to work on Christian. He blew out a breath through his nose and stepped aside reluctantly, allowing Piper, Phoebe, and Paige to get by and make their way out the door. Piper shot a grateful glance at Tessa over her shoulder, but Tessa was busy whispering to Taryn, running her hand comfortingly over her sister's hair.

"Wow. Go, Tessa," Paige said once they were free and clear of the dining hall.

"He probably realized what a jerk he was being, when Tessa and Taryn had just found out their sister was dead," Phoebe said, crossing her arms over her chest.

It was so windy out now that Piper's long hair whipped around her face, stinging her skin as she, Phoebe, and Paige huddled together and rushed along the dirt paths to their tent. The moment they ducked inside, Piper plopped down on her cot and let out a loud sigh.

"Well, at least it's over," she said, pushing her tangled mass of hair behind her shoulders. She bent at her waist and pulled her suitcase out from under her cot, jimmying it between her feet and into the center of the floor. She flung open the top flap and started to organize the rumpled clothes inside, making room for the rest of her stuff.

"What're you doing?" Phoebe asked, her forehead creased.

"Packing," Piper responded, folding a T-shirt over her arm. "We did what we came here to do. We can go home now."

She saw Paige and Phoebe look at each other warily but pretended not to notice. Instead she started grabbing clothing that had ended up hanging from the various furniture in the room, and folding it up. There was no way she was going to let her little sisters talk her into staying now. No way.

"Piper, come on," Paige said, walking over and taking a T-shirt right out of Piper's hands. "Now that we got rid of the kidnappers, we can have an actual vacation!"

"Paige, this isn't a vacation!" Piper said. "It's a nuthouse! Besides, most of the nuts have already left. There are no Wiccans left to be all Wiccan with!"

"I bet some of them come back now that we've vanquished the Anubi," Phoebe said. "Word travels fast, right? And they're not going to want to miss the rededication ceremony. It's kind of a big deal."

Piper leveled her sister with a stare. "You mean *they* think it's kind of a big deal, right?" she demanded.

Phoebe looked away and bit her bottom lip.

"Oh, come on, Phoebe! Tell me you're not into this!" Piper exclaimed, tossing a pair of jeans into her bag.

"Hey! I spent a lot of time and energy on that piece for the rededication ceremony," Phoebe half whined. "I don't want to leave before it gets read!"

"It's two against one, Piper," Paige said, standing next to Phoebe and folding her arms over the front of her ruffled blouse. "What do you say?"

Piper pressed her lips together and looked from Paige to Phoebe, hoping one of them would show some sign of cracking. One little trace of uncertainty. But they didn't. They both were clearly resolved to see this Gathering of the Covens thing through.

"All right, fine, but for our next vacation we're going to Aruba or something," she said firmly. She kicked her suitcase back under her cot and lay down as Phoebe and Paige started figuring out what they were going to wear for the ceremony.

Please! Piper thought. *If I get through this night without laughing my butt off, it'll be a miracle.*

Sitting in a circle before the bonfire with the rest of the covens that evening, Paige felt an overwhelming sense of joy and peace. The clouds had cleared out and the dark sky was filled with a million flickering stars. The wind was still kicking, blowing the flowers that decorated the altar and the circle all over the place, but no one seemed to care much. A few of the covens that had fled earlier in the week had returned, and everyone had dressed up for the occasion. Most of the women wore flowers in their hair, and some of the men wore horned helmets. Even Jasmine's coven had gotten a little colorful in the spirit of the summer solstice, wearing purple and red scarves and crystal jewelry.

Paige herself had worn a billowing purple peasant top and had woven yellow and white blooms through her French braid. Phoebe had done the same with her hair, and even Piper, after a lot of cajoling, had agreed to a few flowers of her own, though she had insisted on wearing jeans.

"This is so cool," Paige said, leaning in toward Piper's ear.

"Yeah. What's the point of this again?" Piper asked in a whisper.

Paige rolled her eyes. "We're dedicating ourselves to the spiritual path of Wicca and to the Goddess," she replied. "And if you laugh, I'll kick your butt."

Piper simply smiled and sat up straight again, turning her attention to Marcia.

Marcia read the Rededication Rite at the altar, which was decorated with a white cloth and yellow candles. Every coven had contributed its own passage, but it all flowed together as if it were one piece. Marcia, for the first time since

Paige met her, looked calm, if a bit tired. She was wearing a wreath on her head, with ribbons tumbling down her back, and a white off-the-shoulder gown. Her voice was confident and comforting at the same time. Paige couldn't have been more happy that she and her sisters had stayed for this. She had a feeling it was a night she was going to remember for the rest of her life.

"I'm getting tired," Piper said with a huge yawn, checking her watch. "You think it's almost over?"

"Piper!" Phoebe hissed, whacking her sister's arm. "I think we're almost up to my passage."

"Besides, after this we get cakes and ale," Paige put in, raising her eyebrows.

"Cakes and ale, huh?" Piper said with an impressed frown. "All right. I'll stick around."

Paige grinned, and just as she returned her attention to Marcia, Phoebe reached past Piper to tap her knee.

"This is it! This is my part!" she said giddily.

"Blessed Lady, on this night we thank thee
For all those who have come into our lives
    through your love,
For all those who share with us your wis-
    dom and your light,
For all the fruits of your strength and
    power

And for the promise of the gifts yet to
    come.
We thank thee humbly for granting us
    peace on this night.
Peace without and peace within. . . ."

"That was it!" Phoebe announced in a whisper, beaming as Marcia continued to read.

"Phoebe, I'm impressed!" Piper said once Marcia was finished. "You have a knack for this stuff."

"Thank you very much," Phoebe replied with a pleased flush.

"All that stuff about peace," Paige said, smiling. "You knew we were gonna catch the bad guys before tonight, didn't ya?"

"More like I was *hoping*," Phoebe said humbly.

Marcia stepped out from behind the altar and raised her palms to the sky. She looked up at the stars, then closed her eyes.

"Lady and Lord, accept our words of devotion on this blessed night," she said. "We thank thee for our faith and dedicate our lives once again to your good name. Let your power live within us throughout the season and throughout the year."

"So mote it be!" Paige exclaimed in unison with the crowd, jumping to her feet along with the rest of the covens.

Piper and Phoebe laughed as everyone stood up and hugged and started to dance. A little band of musicians from the hippie coven, who had returned late that afternoon, struck up some minstrel-style music, and the dancing only grew wilder. Piper and Phoebe stood up, and Paige grabbed their hands, whipping them around in a circle. Phoebe laughed, and even Piper couldn't contain herself and was soon laughing as well.

"Cakes and ale!" someone shouted. Paige whirled to see that Christian and the rest of his coven were wheeling out tables filled with fruit and luscious-looking breads and cakes. Someone started to pass out cups, and soon the wine was flowing as well.

"This is like a prettier version of a frat party," Phoebe said, taking a cup of wine for herself.

"Nothing wrong with that," Piper said, loading up a plate with food.

"So, Piper, I didn't see Tessa and Taryn tonight," Paige said.

"Yeah, they left a couple of hours ago," Piper replied with a sigh. "Tessa said they were just exhausted and they wanted to get home."

"I hope they'll be okay," Phoebe put in. "I felt so badly for them this afternoon. I almost didn't think Taryn was going to make it when she heard that all the witches were dead."

"I know, but they'll be all right eventually. It's just going to take time," Piper said. "For now I think we should just try to have a good time tonight. I think they would want us to."

"Hey, girls!" a voice called out over the crowd.

Paige turned to find Jasmine walking up to them, her curly hair blowing all over the place in the wind. She had dusted her face with a light coating of silvery purple glitter and had drawn a tiny star next to her right eye. Paige had never seen her look so beautiful.

"Hey!" Paige said. "You should stray from the all-black thing more often."

"Oh . . . thanks," Jasmine said, her eyes bright. She held up a plate full of snacks. "Did you try this raisin bread yet? It's unreal."

"Not yet," Paige said.

She glanced around for her sisters, looking for a way to get out of this conversation quickly and gracefully, but Piper and Phoebe had wandered closer to the bonfire. Paige hoped Jasmine didn't want to talk about their powers again and that she wasn't still angry about Piper's freezing her earlier that day. The last thing any of them needed was a public airing of magical laundry.

"So, did you like the ceremony?" Jasmine asked, taking a bite of her bread.

"Yeah, it was very cool," Paige replied. "What did you think? You guys have probably done it up better in the past, huh?"

"No! I really liked it!" Jasmine said with a nod as she looked around at the crowd. "I have to say, I'm impressed. I thought it was going to be all schlocky and hokey, but Marcia knows her stuff. I mean, I take these rituals *very* seriously, so it's hard to impress me."

"Ah," Paige said with a small smile. Sometimes Jasmine's ego was a little too prevalent. But at least she was talking about something other than what had gone on that afternoon.

"So, I know you guys weren't going to see the tigers this afternoon," Jasmine said, a knowing smile in her eyes.

Paige gave herself a mental kick. She knew that the moment she got comfortable, Jasmine would bring it up. What was wrong with her?

"What did Tessa and Taryn tell you?" Paige asked, walking a few feet away from the crowd so that they wouldn't be overheard.

"Not much. Just that you guys found the kidnappers and dealt with them," Jasmine said with a shrug. "Don't worry about it, P., your secret's safe with me. I've got powers, too, you know. When you've got 'em, you like to use 'em."

Paige nodded thoughtfully. There Jasmine went again, alluding to her power. Was she just talking about the parlor tricks she and her friends had played the other night, or did she have some actual sizzle up her sleeves?

"What kind of powers, exactly?" Paige asked nonchalantly. "Anything cool?"

"Oh, nothing like what you guys can do,

obviously," Jasmine said, glancing over her shoulder at Piper and Phoebe, who were starting to dance with some of the hippie guys. "No, you three are special. . . ."

Paige was surprised by Jasmine's words. It was the first almost-humble thing she'd said since they met.

"I'd show you, but I wouldn't want to freak out these wanna-bes," Jasmine added, turning to face Paige again, her curls flying. She took a sip of her drink and smiled conspiratorially. "You understand," she said.

"Of course," Paige replied, trying not to smirk.

"Don't worry, though. I'm honing my powers right now, but I'll show you what I can do," Jasmine said, lifting her cup to her lips again, "when the time comes."

For some reason a chill ran down Paige's arms at these last words. What exactly did Jasmine mean when she said she was "honing" her powers? Maybe she was more powerful than Paige originally believed. Paige looked into Jasmine's eyes, and the smile there had somehow darkened. But then she blinked and the shadow was gone. Paige cleared her throat and looked away. Had she imagined it?

"Well, I gotta go save Chloe," Jasmine said. "The girl gets messy when there's ale around. It's *so* embarrassing. And we do have a reputation to uphold."

"What reputation is that?" Phoebe asked.

"We take our magic seriously," Jasmine replied firmly. "Our coven is one of the elite covens on the East Coast, and I haven't let Chloe's alcoholic tendencies get in the way of that yet."

Suddenly a loud whoop went out from the other side of the bonfire, and Paige looked up to see Purple Hair herself being swung around and off her feet by one of Christian's brethren.

"Then, you'd better go to it," Paige said.

Jasmine paled and shoved her plate and cup at Paige, then took off in Chloe's direction.

As Jasmine flitted off, Paige laughed and waved her few free fingers, pushing her unease aside. Jasmine was just Jasmine, whatever powers she might have. All the girl was interested in was being the coolest girl at the ball—or the coolest Wiccan at the Gathering, in this case.

"Paige, come on!" Phoebe called out from the midst of the evergrowing number of dancing Wiccans. "Piper is actually skipping!"

This Paige had to see. She jogged over to join her sisters by the band, forgetting all about Jasmine's temporary darkness. The kidnappers were vanquished and she was officially here for pleasure, not business. It was time to let her Wiccan hair down!

• • •

That night Piper jolted awake in a panic, suddenly unable to breathe. Fear gripped her heart before she was even fully awake—before she could even open her eyes. She felt the hand over her mouth just before her own hands were wrenched behind her and tied tightly with a length of rope that burned her skin. Piper flailed wildly, trying to get a look at her assailants, but they were behind her, tying her up, gagging her with some kind of cloth.

Grunting as loudly as she could, Piper looked at her sisters, who were somehow sleeping soundly through her struggle. How could they not hear this? How could they not wake up? Just the sound of her pulse roaring in her ears was loud enough to wake the dead. She kicked out, trying to knock something over or hit something hard, but there wasn't much in the tent to destroy, and her powers were useless with her hands tied.

This can't be happening! It can't be! Piper thought, her mind racing as she struggled. *We vanquished you! You're dead! The kidnappers are dead!*

Piper's heart pounded furiously as she was dragged backward from the tent, kicking and flailing to no avail. *Wake up! Please just wake up, one of you!* Piper cried soundlessly. Phoebe and Paige didn't move a muscle. Piper stared helplessly at her sisters through tear-blurred eyes until the tent flap closed in front of her and blocked them from view. Everything happened so quickly Piper wasn't even sure they would have had time to react even if they *had* woken up.

The moment the kidnappers got Piper outside, she used all the strength left in her body to pull herself away, wheeling around in a circle from the force of her own motion. Hands tied, mouth gagged, she whipped her hair out of her face and got one good look at her captors.

"Oh, my God," Piper said through her gag. *It can't be. . . .*

Then everything went black.

Chapter

11

"Paige! Paige, wake up!"

"Phoebe?" Paige muttered, slinging her forearm across her face to shield her eyes as she blinked them open. Harsh sunlight was already streaming into the tent, but Paige felt as if she'd been asleep for only a couple of hours. She was sweating like crazy, and she kicked her blankets away from her.

"What's wrong?" Paige asked groggily as she sat up. It was clear from Phoebe's panicked tone that something had happened, but Paige was still half asleep, and the moment she was upright, a sharp pain shot through her forehead. "Ugh . . . too much ale," she groaned.

"Forget the ale," Phoebe said sharply. "Paige, Piper's gone!"

"What?!" Paige opened her eyes fully for the

first time and looked across the tent at Piper's cot. Her eyes watered immediately from the sting of the direct sunlight, but Paige could see that Piper's sheets were tangled and twisted. The top sheet trailed across the floor, and her pillow was at the foot of her bed.

"Well, maybe she just got up in a rush," Paige said, standing and walking over to her sister's cot, ignoring the throbbing in her head. "I mean, she wasn't taken, right? We vanquished the Anubi."

"I don't know, Paige. I have a really bad feeling about this," Phoebe said, wringing her hands. "It's *really* not like Piper to leave such a mess. And it's only seven o'clock in the morning. When was the last time she got up before seven o'clock?"

"Okay, just stay calm. Let's think this through," Paige said. Her pulse was starting to pound and she brought both hands up to press them against her forehead. This couldn't be happening. There was no way Piper could have been taken. They had solved this whole thing *yesterday*!

"If she struggled, why didn't we wake up?" Paige asked, grasping at straws. "Why didn't she just use her powers and blow something up, or blow up whatever took her?"

"Maybe she couldn't, I don't know," Phoebe said, sitting on the edge of her bed. "But all those other people who had coven members kidnapped said no one heard a thing. And we did have a few cups of that wine last night, so we were probably totally out." She paused and took a deep breath, thinking. "Paige, what if the Anubi didn't take all those other Wiccans? What if the kidnapper is still out there and he has Piper now?"

"But we put a protection spell on the tent!" Paige cried, starting to feel desperate. "There's no way anyone could have gotten past . . ."

Paige trailed off as a suspicion started to take shape in her mind. Fear gripped her stomach like a vise and she sat down on Piper's bed, almost unable to breathe. She clutched Piper's cold pillow, trying to get control of her racing brain.

"What is it?" Phoebe asked, her brow creasing. "What's wrong?"

"Jasmine," Paige said, her voice coming out in a whisper. "She said something to me last night . . . oh, God, this is not good."

"What?" Phoebe wailed, standing up. "Paige, tell me!"

"She said she was honing her powers and that she would show them to me when the time came," Paige blurted out. "It sounded so menacing at the time, but then I thought it was just Jasmine being Jasmine—"

"So maybe this is what she meant by showing

you," Phoebe said. "Maybe she took Piper."

"And she said that thing the other night about Craig getting what he deserved. . . ." Paige squeezed her eyes shut, confused by a jumble of thoughts. "I don't know, maybe she was helping the Anubi or something."

"And she could have gotten past our spell last night because she wasn't beyond our trust," Phoebe added. "I mean, she's annoying, but we were friendly with her."

Paige stood up, shaking from head to toe. "Phoebe, I could have prevented this. I should have told you guys what she said last night."

"Paige, it's not your fault," Phoebe said, reaching out to take Paige's hand. "No one would ever have thought she was the kidnapper. We thought we *killed* the kidnappers."

"But Piper wanted to go home last night, and I whined until she said she'd stay," Paige continued, her eyes welling up with tears. "If we had just gone home . . ."

"I did some whining of my own," Phoebe said. She squeezed Paige's hand and looked her in the eye. "There's nothing we could have done, but there's something we can do now. Let's go find Jasmine."

Paige crossed the room and shoved her feet into her sandals, then she and Phoebe took off across the campground, still dressed in their pajamas. The camp was just starting to stir, but

Paige barely noticed that there was anyone else around. She just hoped and prayed that Jasmine hadn't cleared out yet. That girl had some serious explaining to do.

Jasmine's side of the campground was completely still and silent. Many of the covens that had pulled out of this area of the camp hadn't come back for the festival. Phoebe pushed aside the flap door to Jasmine's tent, and Paige walked right in. She paused for a moment inside the door, stunned. The tent was a complete wreck. There was a circle of melted candles at the foot of Chloe's bed, which was right in the center of the room. The colorful wax had streamed together and hardened into a swirling pool right at Paige's feet. There were clothes and scarves and beads strewn everywhere, and crushed cups from the celebration littered the floor.

Chloe was asleep with her head at the foot of the bed, snoring loudly. Annie was in a cot on the right side of the room, turned toward the wall. Paige glanced at the cot to the left, caught a glimpse of Jasmine's curly hair, and walked right over to her. The girl was wearing a black satin eye mask, and her curls were spread perfectly over the pillow.

"Jasmine!" Paige said loudly, not caring if she woke the whole camp. "Wake up, we need to talk to you!"

Chloe groaned in her sleep on the center cot,

rolled over, and pulled her blanket over her head, probably coping with a serious hangover.

"Jasmine!" Paige shouted again, hovering over the girl's bed.

This time Jasmine sat up straight so fast Paige had to jump back. Jasmine whipped her eye mask from her face and blinked against the sunlight.

"What's going on?" she asked, glaring at Phoebe and Paige. "What the hell are you doing in my tent?"

"What the hell were you doing in *our* tent last night?" Paige shot back.

Annie stirred and looked over at the trio, confused. "What's going on?" she asked, pushing her straight hair away from her face as she lifted her head from the pillow.

"We just want to ask Jasmine about her powers," Phoebe replied, crossing her arms over her chest. Paige marveled at the fact that her sister could look threatening even in light blue cloud pajama pants and a tiny white tank top.

"My powers?" Jasmine asked, narrowing her eyes indignantly. "You woke me up at this ungodly hour to ask about my powers?"

"Yeah, is one of them the ability to silently kidnap innocent people in the middle of the night?" Paige demanded.

"Is someone else missing?" Jasmine asked, fear lighting her eyes as she held her hand to her chest.

Paige looked at Phoebe. That seemed like pretty genuine emotion. But still, the girl could just be a good actress.

"Nice try," Paige said. "You better show us what you can do right now, or we're going straight to the police."

"The police?" Jasmine repeated.

"Or maybe we'll just deal with you in our own way," Phoebe added, looking down her nose at Jasmine. Paige knew that Phoebe would never hurt Jasmine unless she absolutely had to, but the idle threat seemed to work.

Jasmine pushed herself out of bed, the hem of her long black nightgown tumbling to the floor, and lifted her chin. "Can I please speak to you outside?" she asked. Then she swept past Phoebe and Paige and out the door of the tent. Paige couldn't believe the girl had the gall basically to give orders at a time like this. Didn't she realize when she was snagged?

When Paige and Phoebe walked outside, Jasmine turned to them with a completely new expression on her face. Gone was the cockiness and the confidence, replaced by fear and desperation. She reached out and pulled Phoebe and Paige by the wrists until they were all a few yards away from her tent. Then she checked over each shoulder quickly, scanning the deserted camp area. When she looked at Paige again, she tucked her chin close to her chest, so that her hair fell over her face.

"I don't have any powers," she said so quietly Paige could barely hear her.

"What?" Paige demanded, her eyes wide. "What was all that crap last night about *honing* and . . . and not wanting to scare the wanna-be freaks?"

Jasmine let out a pathetic, indignant squeak and tipped her head back. "I was just . . . I don't know. I just . . . "

"You wanted us to think you had power so we'd think you were cool," Phoebe said bluntly.

"Like I care if you guys think I'm cool," Jasmine spit back.

Phoebe raised one eyebrow at her and stared her down until she cracked.

"Fine, if that's the way you want to put it," Jasmine said, shaking her head and rolling her eyes as if Phoebe had just accused her of something she *didn't* do. "But everyone in my coven thinks that I do, so don't tell anyone, okay?"

"But what about what you said the other night about Craig getting what he deserved?" Paige asked desperately, ignoring Jasmine's plea. Part of her wanted Jasmine to be the culprit. At least she was standing right in front of them and she was something they could deal with. If Jasmine hadn't taken Piper, then they were going to be completely lost.

"You think *I* had something to do with Craig's death?" Jasmine spit out, shocked. "Wasn't he, like, drained of all his blood? I mean, eeeew!"

Paige and Phoebe exchanged a look. This girl was just too much.

"I just said that because Craig totally hit on me our first night here," Jasmine continued. "He was completely gross."

"Can't say I disagree with that one," Phoebe said under her breath. "Though he *obviously* didn't deserve to be killed for being a pig."

"I don't believe this," Paige said, throwing up her hands. Tears of frustration threatened to spill over, and she turned away from Jasmine so she wouldn't see and ask a million questions. Paige didn't have time for a million questions from the biggest fake wanna-be of them all. She had to find her sister.

"Come on, Paige, let's go," Phoebe said, wrapping her arms around Paige's back and turning her away from Jasmine's tent.

"You guys won't tell anyone, right?" Jasmine called after them. "About my . . . powers?"

"Whatever," Paige said. Jasmine's rep was the last thing on her mind right now. There was only one thought dominating her brain as she and Phoebe made their way back to the tent. If Jasmine hadn't taken Piper, then who had?

• • •

"Okay, I'm at a loss. I have no idea who's doing this," Phoebe said as she followed Paige back into their tent. She glanced at Piper's bed and then immediately turned away. Just looking at it made her sick. She could practically see Piper struggling, see the fear in her eyes. It just made Phoebe want either to sit down and cry, or to punch something really hard. But at the moment neither of those options was going to help them.

"We have to call Leo," Paige said, picking up Piper's pillow.

"He's going to lose it," Phoebe said, her heart pounding rapidly in her chest. She couldn't even think about how Leo would react when he heard this news. It made her chest hurt even worse than it already did.

Against her will, Phoebe looked at Piper's bed again, and something deep inside of her snapped. She walked over and snatched Piper's pillow from Paige's hands, intending to straighten the bed so that the evidence of the struggle wouldn't be right there in her face anymore. But the moment she touched Piper's pillow, she was seized with a vivid vision.

Piper was on her knees, her hands tied behind her back, and her mouth gagged with a long red cloth. She was in the middle of a circle of similarly gagged and tied people, all of whom were consumed by fear. The fear was so great Phoebe could practically taste it. An altar was being prepared at the front of a large room, with black candles, a bowl of some kind, and lengths of purple and black gauze. Suddenly Piper's eyes opened in fear, and Phoebe saw someone approaching her sister with a large, glinting knife. . . .

"Oh, my God," Phoebe said, snapping out of her vision. She grabbed on to Paige's arm for support before her knees went out from under her. Her head was swimming, and for a split second she was sure she was going to faint, but she held on. She had to stay focused. If she didn't, Piper was going to die.

"What did you see?" Paige asked, helping Phoebe to Piper's bed.

Phoebe sat down, trembling, still clutching Piper's pillow with one hand. "Some kind of ritual," Phoebe said. "There were a lot of witches and someone with a huge knife." She looked at Paige, squeezing her arm tightly. "He's going to kill Piper," she said.

"All right, that's it," Paige said. "Leo! Leo! Get your butt down—"

Before she could finish her rant, Leo appeared in front of them in a swirl of white and blue sparkles.

"What's up?" he asked casually, looking around. "Everything okay?"

"No, Leo, everything is not okay," Paige said, trying to sound calm. "Maybe you should sit down."

"Why?" Leo asked, freezing. Then realization dawned in his blue eyes. "Did something happen to Piper? Where is she?"

"She was kidnapped sometime in the middle of the night, Leo," Phoebe said, pressing her hands into her thighs. "I'm sorry. We didn't hear anything."

"Wait a minute, she was *kidnapped*?" Leo blurted out. "But you guys vanquished those—"

"We know," Paige said. "But apparently there's another kidnapper out there. Someone who wants to perform some kind of ritual."

"What are you talking about?" Leo asked. "How do you know this?"

"Because I had a vision," Phoebe said, avoiding eye contact with him. "Someone has a lot of witches . . . including Piper . . . and he's going to kill them all."

All the blood drained from Leo's face as he took in this information. "I'm going to her," he said. "She hasn't been taken to the underworld. I can sense her."

He started to orb out, but Paige jumped up and stopped him. "Wait!" she shouted, causing his white lights to stop swirling. "We're going with you. You don't know what you could be orbing into. You may need the Power of Three."

"Fine," he said, pulling Paige to him. He looked down at Phoebe and held out his hand. "Let's go," he said firmly. "I just hope we're not too late."

Somehow Phoebe managed to get to her feet and take Leo's hand. She was still shaky from the vision, but she knew what she had to do. She had to get her strength back. It was the only hope Piper had.

She wrapped her arms around Leo, and the three of them orbed off.

Chapter

12

The moment Phoebe's feet hit solid ground, she widened her stance and raised her arms, ready to take out anyone who stood in her way, fear-fueled adrenaline rushing through her veins. But when she got a look around, her taut muscles relaxed a bit. She, Paige, and Leo were standing in a tight passageway, surrounded by huge, hulking shelves filled with wooden crates. The shelves stretched as high as the ceiling, which seemed to be miles overhead, and the smell of sawdust thickened the air. There wasn't a soul in sight.

"Where are we?" Paige asked, confused as she eyed the crates. She walked past Phoebe, running her fingers along one of the steel shelves and coming up with a thick layer of dust. "Ugh," she grunted, wiping her hands together to clean them. "Whatever it is, it hasn't been cleaned in a while."

"It's some kind of warehouse," Leo said. He lightly touched the rough surface of the nearest crate and looked at Phoebe. "So, where is everyone?"

"This can't be right," Phoebe said, tilting her head back. "The warehouse I saw was huge and empty. I don't remember any of this stuff."

Suddenly Phoebe heard a voice as low as a whisper, and her heart caught. She raised one finger to tell the others to be silent and listened closely. Soon enough it came again. One low but powerful voice. It seemed to be coming from the other side of the crates to her left.

"Follow me," she whispered.

The sneakers she'd slipped on that morning made no sound as she crept along the passageway. Phoebe looked down at her feet and realized both she and Paige were still in their pajamas— not exactly the most menacing clothing, or the most practical for a fight, but they would have to do. She paused as she came to the edge of the shelves. Moving as slowly as possible, she looked around the crates. She could tell that on the other side of these shelves the room opened up, but she still couldn't see anything.

The voice, however, was louder now. They were getting closer. Phoebe pressed her back up against the crates at the end of the shelf. Leo and

Paige did the same, then they edged their way along until they came to the corner. Phoebe's palms were sweating as she flattened them against the splinter-riddled crate behind her.

"Okay, nobody move," she whispered.

Phoebe took one peek around the side of this last row of crates and froze. A huge area of the warehouse had been cleared and was set up for the ritual she had seen in her vision. But there was an added detail she hadn't seen—Christian was standing against the far left wall, his hands behind his back, wearing a tight black T-shirt and looking around the room with an expression Phoebe would never have thought possible on his normally sweet face.

He looked threatening—even evil. He looked like he was in charge.

The rest of his coven lined the walls, each in the same position as Christian, each a few feet away from the next man. Their faces were set like stone as they glared at the circle of bound Wiccans before them.

"It's Christian," Phoebe whispered, reaching her hand out to clutch Paige's. "He must be the one who's doing all this."

"Christian? How is that possible?" Paige said.

"I have no idea," Phoebe replied, her mind racing. Christian had seemed so surprised when she told him about the whole most-powerful-Wiccan aspect of the kidnappings. He'd seemed concerned. Was he just that good of an actor? And what did Craig's death and the Anubi have to do with all of this? It was all too much to take in.

"Do you see Piper?" Leo asked.

"Not yet," Phoebe replied.

Sixteen witches were arranged in a large circle, each on his or her knees and each gagged, just as Phoebe had seen in her premonition. Their hands were tied tightly behind their backs with thick lengths of rope. They were not blindfolded, so most of them were looking around the room wildly as if they were anticipating something awful. A red-haired girl closest to Phoebe was silently weeping. She looked pale and weak, and Phoebe wondered if she was one of the first Wiccans taken. How long had Christian and his friends been holding her?

Piper was nowhere in sight, but Phoebe saw Keisha—the witch she had heard about when she and her sisters had questioned Wiccans for Daryl—kneeling on the opposite side of the circle. Her dark skin was covered in a sheen of perspiration and she seemed to be looking right at Phoebe. Suddenly Phoebe recalled that Keisha could see through solid objects, and she shook her head ever so slightly, trying to tell the girl not to give them away. Keisha immediately looked down at the concrete floor, but not before Phoebe saw the hope in her eyes.

There was a black candle on the floor between each witch, and a pentagram had been painted in red in the center of the circle. The altar Phoebe had seen stood at the far end of the room, decorated with the purple and black cloth. Two people stood on either side of the altar in black hooded cloaks, their backs to the circle and to Phoebe.

"Bring in the final sacrifice," Christian said suddenly, his voice clear and strong.

A group of people emerged from the shadows behind the altar. As they came into the light cast by the candles Phoebe saw that it was two of Christian's brethren and that they were dragging a struggling Piper between them. The more she kicked and pulled, the tighter they seemed to grip her arms, until her face contorted with pain.

"Oh, my God," Phoebe gasped, her grip on Paige tightening.

Leo instantly stepped out from his hiding place to see her, but Paige pulled him back. Phoebe held her breath as her sister struggled all the way to the center of the circle, straining against her gag and wrenching her hands to try to get them free. Her eyes were wet, but she never shed a tear. She was forced onto her knees in the center of the pentagram, and she tossed her hair back from her face defiantly, glaring at the people by the altar.

Maybe I have it wrong. Maybe they're *the ones in charge,* Phoebe thought, turning her attention to the hooded figures. Were they more members of Christian's coven?

"We have to help her," Leo said, straining to remain calm.

Before Phoebe could respond, a powerful female voice filled the room, seeming to infuse the air with its timbre. Phoebe glanced at Paige, surprised. She thought Christian's coven was made up entirely of men.

"We have gathered here for a great purpose," the voice began. "Our ascension will mean the end of eons of clashes, of struggle, of strife. We will bring order to the earth. We will bring the order of hell."

A chill raced over Phoebe's skin and into her heart. The two cloaked figures turned around and swept their hoods from their faces, and Phoebe almost fell to her knees herself.

It was Tessa and Taryn. Their pale, dewy skin seemed to glow in the light of the candles as they stared dead ahead as if entranced. Taryn stood straight and tall, her chin held high, appearing strong and in perfect health. She looked like a completely different person.

"Paige . . . ," Phoebe said, her voice coming out as a squeak.

Paige stretched her neck and looked around the corner for the first time. Just as she did the

speaker stepped out of the shadows and walked
up to the altar. She was dressed in flowing black
and purple robes, her long, straight blond hair
falling over her shoulders like a shimmering
blanket. Her eyes were the exact same piercing
blue as Tessa's and Taryn's. Phoebe had no
doubt in her mind that she was looking at their
little sister, Tina. The one who had supposedly
disappeared.

"Christian *and* Tessa and Taryn?" Paige said
throatily. "But how?"

"We wish to thank you, our Wiccan brothers
and sisters, for making the ultimate sacrifice,"
Tina bellowed, an eerily reverent look in her
eyes as she made eye contact with each and
every one of her victims. "And Piper Halliwell,
our single Charmed One," Tina said, staring
straight at Piper. She stepped out from behind
the altar, her hands folded in front of her. "It
seems you are no longer alone."

Before her words had sunk into Phoebe's reeling mind, Tina looked up, directly into Phoebe's
eyes. Her first instinct was to jump back, but it
was too late. Tina had seen them. Both Paige and
Leo stepped out from their hiding place, and the
three of them stood there defiantly.

"Your sisters have come for you, just as I pre-
dicted," Tina continued, a sneer curling across
her lips. "And your man is here as well! How
sweet." Piper turned her head and looked at

Phoebe, her expression a mixture of relief and anger. Relief that they had found her. Anger that they had put themselves in danger.

"We're glad you could make it, girls," Tina said, opening her arms to her sides. "Once we're done with Piper, you're next."

She glanced at Christian and tossed her hand nonchalantly in Phoebe's direction. "Seize them," she said casually. Then she grinned and clapped her hands together. "I've always wanted to say that!"

"What a wacko," Paige said under her breath, rolling her eyes as a few of Christian's coven members advanced on her, Phoebe, and Leo.

"Tell me about it," Phoebe replied.

"We don't want to hurt you . . . yet," one of the attackers said, approaching Phoebe slowly.

"Well, luckily I don't have the same issues," Phoebe said.

Just as he and another, skinnier guy lunged at Phoebe she vaulted herself into the air, executed a flip over their heads, and came down on her feet behind them. Before they had a chance to turn around, she landed a kick in the small of the first guy's back, sending him sprawling into the skinnier guy.

All at once Damon lunged at Leo, and Leo easily landed a punch to the shorter guy's jaw, sending him reeling backward, but it didn't take long for a few of his friends to come to his aid. Just as a beer-gutted guy grabbed Paige from behind, holding her arms back, three guys managed to do the same to Leo. Paige looked at Leo, then lifted her chin toward the altar.

"Got it," Leo said.

They both disappeared in their swirling lights and reappeared on the far side of the room in opposite corners. Tessa, Taryn, and Tina whirled around to face them, and Paige saw that Damon, the beer-gutted guy, and their friends were all standing near the shelves, confused. Meanwhile, Phoebe head-butted a guy who had managed to get a hold on her from behind, then launched herself into the air and quickly flattened Damon, Beer Gut, and two other men who tried to grab her. So far Christian's coven wasn't turning out to be quite as powerful as his friends had originally boasted.

"Get them!" Tina shouted, pointing at Leo and Paige. Christian and more of his friends moved toward them, and Paige looked at Leo.

"Just get Piper!" she said. "I'll be fine."

Leo orbed out again and reappeared in the center of the circle, where he helped Piper to her feet. He was just untying the rope that held her hands together when Paige's view was blocked by Christian and another meaty coven member.

Christian grabbed her arm and twisted it behind her back, which sent a shooting pain through her shoulder, but Paige refused to let it show in her face.

"Sorry, guys," she said. "See ya!"

Then she orbed out again and reappeared over by Phoebe, who was fighting hand to hand with two men who were having serious trouble with her. The room swirled before Paige's eyes, and she leaned one hand against the shelves, dizzy. She wasn't used to orbing so much in such a short span of time, and it had an effect on her. She pressed her eyes closed, took a deep breath, and opened them to find Beer Gut advancing on her once again.

"Not this time, pal," Paige said. She thrust her palm straight up into his nose and heard a satisfying crack. *That self-defense class I took in college just paid off.*

"You broke my nose!" he shouted, grasping his face as he fell back.

"Baby," Paige said under her breath. Then Phoebe flipped one of her assailants over her back, and he landed at Paige's feet, knocked out.

"Nice one," Paige said. "Need some help?"

"Sure, why not?" Phoebe replied, out of breath. She looked over her shoulder and reeled around, landing a left to one of the guys' jaw and sending him stumbling back a few yards.

Paige wasn't the most experienced fighter,

but she'd watched Phoebe enough to know what worked. As one of the guys turned on her Paige kicked him as hard as she could right in his gut, and when he doubled over, she kneed him in the face. Just as he fell back, stunned, Paige was grabbed from behind again.

"No more disappearing acts," Christian growled in her ear.

"Sorry, Chris," she said. "I can do this all day."

Paige orbed over to the altar again, ready to fight, but the moment she hit ground, she was suddenly flung off her feet and soared through the air. All the air flew from her lungs as she vaulted across the warehouse, flailing helplessly. She didn't even have time to think about orbing before she hit the wall and the wind was knocked right out of her. Pain radiated through every inch of her body. Paige threw her arms out to break her fall as she crumbled to the floor, coughing uncontrollably.

"What the heck was that?" she muttered once she caught her breath.

As she pushed herself up with her hands, mentally scanning her body for broken bones, she felt someone staring at her. She looked up to see that Tina was smirking at her from across the room. The girl turned toward the circle, where Leo and Piper were untying the other Wiccans, and flicked her wrist casually. Suddenly Leo was flying through the air as if he'd just been hit by an invisible cannonball. But at least he had the sense to make himself orb before he was seriously injured. He reappeared next to Phoebe, and then Paige saw something that she couldn't believe.

Phoebe's arms were pulled back and held there—but there was no one behind her. Phoebe struggled and broke free, but the second she whirled around, her jaw snapped back as if she'd been punched. Then her legs went flying out from under her and she hit the floor on her side—hard. Paige pushed herself to her feet, ignoring the protests her many bruises made. What was going on here?

She looked over at Tina and Taryn, who were both laughing as they watched Phoebe attempt to get up. Phoebe was flattened and apparently pinned to the ground. Each time she tried to rise, something shoved her down again.

"What are you doing to her?" Piper shouted.

"Don't look at me," Tina said through her mirth. "It's Tessa. She does so love this trick."

Suddenly Tessa appeared over Phoebe, her foot holding her down at the center of her back. Paige swallowed hard. Tessa had the power to make herself *invisible*? And Tina could toss them across the room with the effort it took to flick her wrist? How was this possible?

Piper rushed over to Phoebe, and Leo dived

into Tessa, tackling her into the shelves full of crates. The moment he did, however, Tessa disappeared, and then Taryn ran across the circle, which was now half broken up, and flipped through the air, heading for Piper. She defied gravity just as easily as Phoebe ever had.

"Piper, look out!" Paige shouted.

Piper ducked, huddling over Phoebe and sending Taryn hurtling past them and into the crates. She crumpled to the floor next to Phoebe and Piper, stunned. Tina glared furiously at Paige and lifted her wrist, but before she could be flung again, Paige orbed over to her sisters and Leo.

"Where's Tessa?" she asked, turning to Leo, who was just getting up.

"I have no idea," he answered.

"What is going on around here?" Piper asked, rising from the floor and pushing her hair out of her face. "What's with all the crazy power?"

"I don't know," Phoebe answered as she brushed herself off. "But I have a feeling that this isn't going to be as easy as vanquishing the Anubi."

Tessa suddenly reappeared next to Tina, and those members of Christian's coven who hadn't yet been knocked out gathered around them. Paige felt her heart pounding rapidly in her chest. This was going to be one hell of a showdown.

"I'm gonna free the rest of the innocents," Leo said. "You deal with your evil twins over there. Sound like a plan?"

"Sounds like a plan to me," Taryn said shrilly.

Paige turned slowly to see Taryn rise from the floor and hover over her and her sisters, her arms outstretched, her eyes burning with hatred.

"Okay," Paige said, "this is really not good."

"Taryn, I'm bored!" Tina called out in a pouty voice. "Can you just deal with them, already, so we can get on with this?"

Piper looked at her sisters and narrowed her eyes. "I really don't like her."

"Join the club," Phoebe said. She rose into the air to the same level as Taryn and curled her hands into fists. "You wanna go?" she said nonchalantly. "Then, let's go."

Taryn threw out her arm, and Phoebe easily blocked her, then landed a punch in the girl's stomach. As they fought, Piper and Paige turned toward the pentagram and saw that Leo had successfully freed most of the captives, who were now fighting Christian's brethren. The place was complete chaos as a full-on battle erupted.

"You know, you people are really screwing up my plans," Tina said, taking a few steps into the melee, which somehow went on around her without harming her or even touching her. She flicked her hair over her shoulder and looked down at her nails as if she was inspecting her manicure. "I hate it when that happens."

She lifted her hand toward Paige, and Paige squealed and orbed out, reappearing right behind Tina. Before either of the sisters could react, Paige thrust out her hand and yelled, "Rope!" One of the lengths of cord that had bound Piper disappeared in a swirl of light and reappeared in Paige's hand. But just as Paige was about to grab Tina's wrists to bind them Tina turned on her and flicked the rope out of Paige's hand with her power.

"Did you really think you could get away with that?" Tina asked, amused.

Then Piper watched as Paige was grabbed from behind by Inviso-Tessa, just as Phoebe had been. Piper couldn't take much more of this. How were they supposed to fight someone they couldn't even see? Suddenly Taryn flew by overhead and landed with a thud at Tina's feet, unconscious. Tina's jaw dropped as she looked at her prone sister, and Phoebe walked up next to Piper.

"One down," she said, clapping her hands together.

"You so didn't want to do that," Tina said. She flicked her wrist and sent Phoebe flying into the far wall, then Paige was suddenly released, and seconds later Piper was being pinned to the ground right in the center of the pentagram, her face flattened into the red paint by an invisible Tessa.

"Why are you resisting so much?" Tina asked, walking over to Piper, looking down at her serenely. Piper managed to turn her head and look at Leo, who was standing near the left wall. The other Wiccans had gathered Christian's men into a group and were standing around them, guarding them. Leo, Paige, and Phoebe all took a step toward Piper, but Tina raised her hand to stop them. "Don't bother," she said. "I'll just keep tossing you around."

Piper looked up to see Paige and Phoebe exchange a glance and stay where they were. Leo stopped as well. Piper was glad of that. The last thing she needed was for both of her sisters and her husband to get crushed trying to save her.

"All we want is to glean the powers from you and from these other witches," Tina continued, walking in a circle around Piper. Piper pulled at her hands, but Tessa had them tightly in her grip, and from what Piper could tell, the girl's knees were digging into her back. "We knew that once we did that . . . and killed you, of course . . . we could take your place. We could be the Charmed Sisters." She paused and kneeled down, her long hair grazing Piper's cheek as she leaned into her ear. A chill of disgust and fear traveled down Piper's spine, and she struggled against Tessa's grip to no avail. "Of course, we won't waste our time saving innocents who mean nothing to us anyway. We will use your powers for that which they were intended—to make all humanity bow to us and cater to our whims. Who knows?" she said, standing again. "Maybe we'll even take over the underworld."

Tina walked over to Taryn's prone body, knelt next to her, and lifted her torso, letting Taryn's head hang back.

"Taryn, honey, wake up," Tina said, smacking her sister's face so hard it made Piper wince. "It's time to kill, and you have to be awake for that."

Okay, if I don't blow this girl to bits, I'm sending her straight to the loony bin, Piper thought.

After a couple more slaps Taryn finally shook herself awake and blinked up at her sister.

"It's time," Tina said, helping Taryn to her feet.

Tina sauntered back over to Piper as Taryn walked shakily to the altar. She slid a huge knife off the top of the altar and brought it over to Tina, holding it out on her palms like it was some kind of blessed sword. After she handed the weapon to her sister, she bowed slightly and took a few steps back.

"Well, it doesn't have all the candles and circles and hoopla, the way I wanted it, but the ritual will still work," Tina said, turning the knife over for inspection and letting the blade glint menacingly in the candlelight. Piper held her breath and closed her eyes as Tina knelt before her again. She couldn't move, and her sisters could do nothing to save her. All Piper could do at that moment was hope that her death would be quick and that Phoebe and Paige would manage to escape.

"Piper!" Phoebe shouted. "No!"

Suddenly Piper felt Tessa flinch. It was only for a split second, but she loosened her grip. A surge of strength rushed through Piper, and she wrenched her eyes open. Using every ounce of energy she had left, she tossed herself over onto her back, sending Tessa flying. Tessa suddenly reappeared and scrambled over to her sisters as Piper pushed herself to her feet. Paige and Phoebe rushed to Piper's side, and the six of them stood there, facing one another down.

Slowly Tina turned around and replaced the knife on the altar. "You can't win," she said, facing them again. She reached out her hands to her sisters, who gripped them firmly. "There is more than one way to skin the Charmed Ones."

The sisters started to recite a spell, and Phoebe rolled her eyes, looking at Piper. "I can't believe you liked these girls," she said, shaking her head.

"Yeah, well, not anymore," Piper replied.

She lifted her hands and Tina's eyes narrowed. "What's she doing?" she asked, breaking off the spell.

"Uh, you can't just keep freezing us," Tessa said. "Sooner or later we're gonna complete the spell."

Piper looked at Phoebe. "What, they don't know what else I can do with my hands?" she asked.

"No, I think they were fake crying and fainting during that demonstration," Phoebe said.

"Huh. Well, lying will get you nowhere," Piper said. With one powerful thrust she blasted the three evil witches into the atmosphere, cutting off their surprised screams.

"Well done," Paige said, leaning against Piper's arm.

"I can't believe it," Phoebe said incredulously. "They did all that work, and they managed to miss the one most important detail—our major firepower." She slung her arm around Piper's shoulders and gave her a little squeeze. "See? You are the most powerful."

"Yeah, well, it didn't stop me from getting kidnapped," Piper said, rubbing at her raw wrists. She flexed her hands and shook out her fingers. "It feels good to have my hands back. All day long all I've been thinking about is sending those witches where they belong."

Suddenly Piper was wrapped up in Leo's arms, and she pressed her face into his shirt, inhaling his fresh, clean scent and trying not to think about the fact that a little while ago she'd been afraid she would never see him again.

"It's over," he whispered into her ear. "Everyone is safe now."

"No thanks to me," Piper said, turning her face so she could speak and resting her cheek against him. "It's a good thing you guys made me stay, or we would never have figured out that there were two sets of kidnappers out there," she said to Phoebe and Paige.

"I guess our whining is good for something," Paige said with a grin.

Piper smirked. "In this case, but don't make a habit of it."

Chapter

13

Leo went off to find a phone and call the police, and Piper and her sisters watched as the kidnapped Wiccans tied up their captors for safekeeping. Christian let out an indignant grunt when Samson, who'd grown some peach fuzz on his normally shaved head since being kidnapped, tied his hands together. Unfortunately for him, his grunting only made Samson tighten the rope.

"Is everyone all right?" Piper asked, joining the victims over by the wall where they were dealing with Christian's coven. "Does anyone need anything?"

"I just want to make some phone calls," Clarissa said with a smile. She walked right up to Piper and enveloped her in a firm hug. "Thank you so much for saving us. I was beginning to lose hope."

"We were glad we could help," Piper said as Clarissa released her. She stepped over to Samson and looked up at him, his impressive frame dwarfing her. "Do you mind if I talk to Christian for a second?" she asked, rubbing at the back of her neck.

"Be my guest," Samson said. He turned Christian around and backed him up until he was touching the wall, then walked off.

"What do you want?" Christian spit as Phoebe and Paige joined her.

"Just want to know what you were thinking," Piper said flatly. "What was in it for you?"

Christian ground his teeth together and glared at the sisters. "Why should I tell you?"

"Well, you're gonna have to tell the police in a few minutes anyway," Phoebe said, leaning her elbow against the wall next to him. "May as well get your story straight. I'm guessing Craig talked you into this, am I right?"

"Yeah, and now he's not even around to take the fall," Christian said through his teeth.

Piper tried to ignore the fact that he was basically saying Craig had left him in the lurch by dying a horrible death. If she wanted to keep him talking, there was no reason to scold the guy for being a major jerk.

"So . . . what, Tina offered you guys something in return for helping them kidnap people?" she asked.

Christian took a deep breath and then tipped his head forward. "Craig and Tina used to go out. She told him that if we helped, we would all be rewarded when she and her sisters took over."

"So you didn't know anything about the Anubi," Phoebe said.

"The *what*?" Christian asked.

"The things that killed Craig," Paige clarified.

"No! That's why we were all so shocked when he disappeared," Christian replied. "Tina assured us we were safe, so when Craig was kidnapped, we didn't know what was going on."

Piper's stomach turned as she looked at her sisters. All that time she had thought that demons had to be responsible for all the kidnappings, but she was wrong. It was three girls—three people she would have dismissed as powerless, fake wanna-bes—who were executing the perfect crime.

"Well, thanks for your time," Piper said, turning away from him.

"Wait! You'll tell the police it wasn't my idea, right?" he called after them. "You'll back me up?"

"We'll see what we can do," Piper said as she walked away, joined by Paige and Phoebe. She didn't even turn to look at him. She couldn't. The sight of him and the thought of everything he, Tessa, Taryn, and Tina had done made her ill.

"So, the Anubi kidnappings and the other kidnappings were totally unrelated," Paige said as they made their way to the other side of the room. "That's why Craig's bed had all the black markings, but none of the other crime scenes did."

"Looks that way," Piper said, blowing out a sigh. She sat down on the floor and leaned up against the cool cinder-block wall. She hadn't realized how tired she was until that very moment. Her whole body seemed to ache as she let herself relax.

"The Anubi must have been here just to feed off the convention," Phoebe said, sitting down next to Piper. "But it was lucky for Tina and her sisters, because it threw the suspicion from them."

"Yeah, once the Anubi were vanquished, they could basically do anything they wanted," Paige said. "God, we even told everyone it was safe to come back to the campground, and meanwhile, we're hanging out with the psychotic kidnappers at mealtime."

"I still can't believe it was them," Piper said, pushing her hands into her hair. "It was Christian and Tessa who took me last night. I was so shocked when I saw them I would probably have passed out even if they hadn't whacked me over the head."

She winced as she passed her hand over the

lump that had formed where Christian had hit her the night before.

"Ow! Are you okay?" Phoebe asked, reaching her hand out tenderly toward the bump.

"Yeah, just don't touch it!" Piper exclaimed, shrinking away. Phoebe pulled her hand back and frowned apologetically. "I guess I deserve it, anyway," Piper said. "Here I was spouting about how powerless all these loser Wiccans were and believing the criminals were actually victims." She looked down at the gritty cement floor.

"Please!" Paige said, finally dropping to the ground at Piper's other side. "Tessa and Taryn came to you with this sob story about their little sister, and you believed them because you wanted to help. There's nothing wrong with that."

"It could've happened to any of us," Phoebe agreed, rubbing Piper's arm. "Their story fit with everyone else's, and they seemed like victims to me."

At that moment the door on the far side of the room was flung open, and at least twenty armed police officers poured in, followed by Leo. As the cops sorted out the victims from the kidnappers Leo walked over to Piper and her sisters. Piper watched as a few of the policemen handed out blankets and food to the victims, who were all incredibly grateful. Clarissa even shrieked when one of the officers handed her a cell phone. Everyone started to call home and let friends and family know that they were okay. Piper felt a smile start to tug at her lips as Keisha grabbed up one of the policemen in a hug.

"See?" Phoebe said, slipping her arm around Piper's shoulders. "We found the kidnapees and they're all fine, *and* we vanquished the Anubi, so they won't be killing any more witches."

"It was like an added bonus," Paige put in.

"Okay, you're right," Piper said, looking at her sisters. "The end result was good."

She slipped her hand into Paige's and gave it a little squeeze. "I just have one small favor to ask," Piper said.

"What's that?" Paige asked, leaning her head on Piper's shoulder.

Piper smirked. "No more family vacations for a good, *long* time."

About the Author

Emma Harrison is an editor-turned-writer who has worked on many series, including Sweet Valley High Senior Year, Roswell High, and Fearless. She never misses an episode of *Charmed*.

DATE WITH
DEATH

As Piper and Leo contemplate parenthood and
Pheobe and Cole enjoy their engagement,
Paige is feeling more of a push to find a significant
other. In a moment of whimsy, she signs up for
an online dating service. Needless to say, she soon
finds herself flooded with eager responses.
Almost every night she embarks on a new date
that seems to lead nowhere – despite the fact that
Paige has a perfectly good time when she's out.

Or does she? Before long, the sisters discover
that Paige spends her "dates" in a catatonic trance –
she hasn't actually gone anywhere!
Soon afterward, her suitors are discovered to have
committed evil acts. Paige is acting as a conduit
for dark powers – and soon she is projecting
her energies onto her sisters.
Will Piper and Pheobe be able to save her
using only the Power of Two?